incident at the border

by

nick nelson

Illustrations by konrad kraus

ISBN: 978-1-691-61397-7

contents

1. birthday boy

mother smith had a new baby every year on november 1, and as there was room for only eighteen people (including herself) in her little white house, each child on its seventeenth birthday had to leave home and find its own way in the world.

today it was joe's turn. joe had always been a cheerful child, though not very bright or curious, and unlike many of his predecessors had never studied much or given much thought as to what he would do when he was released from the white house.

on the big day (for him) joe got up with the rest of the family at six o'clock, but in honor of the occasion of his departure he was not assigned any "chores" as his previous chore of feeding the pigs had now passed to his brother eddie, who had become fifteen years old.

so joe just lay in bed until breakfast time, staring at the low ceiling of the room he had shared with the three other oldest boys, and wondering what life held in store for him in the great wide world.

the other three were at their assigned tasks - their new assigned tasks, as each had moved up one spot on the duty roster - and the house was somewhat quiet, except for the plaintive crying of the newborn baby, adelaide, and the sound of bacon sizzling in the kitchen.

there was a knock on the door.

"come in," said joe, and the door opened and his sisters teresa and gaia entered.

teresa had just turned sixteen and gaia fourteen. they were the two oldest females in the house except of course for mother who had no age, and joe had always gotten along very well with both of them.

"good morning, joe," said gaia and teresa in unison.

"good morning," joe replied.

"i hope you slept well, " said gaia, "in the night before your big day."

"i do not know if it as big as all that," joe replied with a smile, "after all it must happen to everybody who passes through this world."

"true that," agreed teresa, "but look here, joe, i have brought you something to take with you as you begin your travels. i know you have always expressed a sincere appreciation of my chocolate cupcakes, so here are a dozen of them, neatly wrapped in aluminum foil, and placed in a plain brown bag.,"

"why, thank you so much!" joe exclaimed. "these will really hit the spot, especially as it seems to be a cool day, and i am sure to work up an appetite walking along the road to the city."

"i hope you have room in your bag for them," said teresa, with a smile.

"oh, do not worry about that," replied joe. "that reminds me, i had better start packing, as i do not want to outstay my welcome, in this house in which i have spent my entire existence up to now."

"so," said gaia, "you have decided to head for the city , hey, and not deep into the country? what decided you, if you do not mind my asking?"

"i flipped a coin," said joe, "as i could not decide any other way. i am sure either choice would have been good."

"and wherever did you get a coin?" asked gaia.

"i found it about a week ago, when i was feeding the pigs. the wind must have blown it into the yard. i do not know where it came from, or what it is worth or what country it is a coin of, but i hope it will bring me luck."

"speaking of things that might bring you luck, joe, i too have a present for you, " said gaia, "and one that will not take up too much space in your bag or even in your pocket."

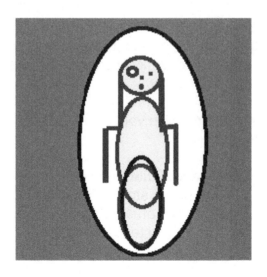

and with that gaia handed joe a little wooden figurine that she had carved, a plain unpainted figure of a woman with one large eye and one small eye, staring vacantly into space, or at some distant horizon.

joe would much have preferred something edible, but as he was well brought up, like all the smith children, he did not say so, but replied, ""thank you so much gaia, i am sure it will bring me all the luck in the world, unlike the coin i found among the pigs, which might portend anything or nothing."

"well, joe," said gaia, changing the subject, "things will be different with you gone, and eddie moving up to number one boy, and even more so with sal moving up to number two boy, as i have always thought him a somewhat devious rascal, with thoughts that are a mystery to all."

"oh, sal is all right," said joe, "he has a good heart under his somewhat mysterious exterior and i am sure everything will go on as it always has."

"we had best be getting along now," said teresa, "as it is a busy time wth the new baby and so many of us assuming new duties, so we will leave you now with a final good luck."

"good luck to you, too," said joe. "and to mother and everybody else."

with that teresa and gaia left the room and closed the door behind them, leaving joe to his packing and to his thoughts.

2. starting out

it was a nice day, and mother smith was sitting outside in her favorite chair.

she was not exactly watching the world go by, as her house was up on a hill, and the road to the city was obscured by a row of trees, but she was staring into the void, as was her accustomed way, thinking her own thoughts, whatever those may have been.

joe emerged from the house, with his suitcase. children leaving the house on their seventeenth birthday were given a choice of a suitcase or a backpack to carry away such belongings as they had and wished to take with them. 76 percent chose the backpack, but joe was among the 23 percent who opted for the suitcase. (one percent chose neither.)

joe's suitcase was hastily and lightly packed, and not too heavy. in his pocket were two of the chocolate cupcakes teresa had given him, as well as some loose change he had saved, and the lucky coin he had found while tending the pigs.

"good morning, mother," said joe.

"good morning, joe," mother replied. "i see you have a nice day to begin your travels. i remember when matilda left last year it was pouring rain, so you may consider yourself fortunate."

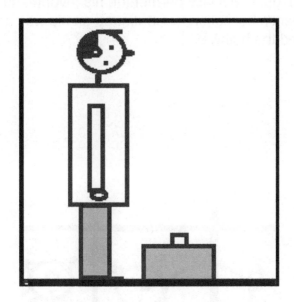

"indeed i do," said joe. he looked down the hill. "i can never remember which way is the city and which is the country, although i have been told several times."

"i believe there is a sign on the highway," said mother, "but in any case if you go left you will head into the city and if you go right you will go into the countryside."

"thank you," said joe. "that should not be too difficult to remember. good-bye, mother. thank you for bringing me into this world. "

"it was my pleasure. good-bye, joe."

joe started down the hill. the path was clearly marked, and he reached the bottom of the hill safely.

he remembered that he had forgotten to say good-bye to the pigs, especially parmenter, his favorite, but after a monent's hesitation he continued on his way and reached the highway.

but he had forgotten again which direction the city was in, and he did not see the sign that mother had described.

of course nobody in the world cared which direction he took.

joe started walking.

as he walked along he wondered what sort of person he would first encounter.

a vampire? a billionaire? a movie star? a serial killer or homicide detective? a world famous novelist or movie director? a mad preacher or guru?   a trained deadly assassin? a lone wolf dispensing solitary justice? joe was familiar with all these types from watching television in the evenings with mother and the other children after finishing his chores.

or would he first meet just an ordinary person like himself, wandering the earth?

finally he came to the sign mother had told him about.

he was heading in the direction of the city.

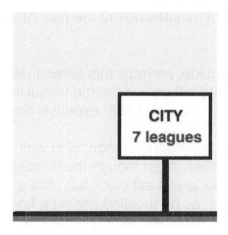

3. magnus

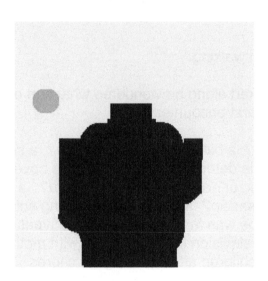

the first person joe encountered on the road was not
walking towards him, towards the country, but ahead
of him, towards the city.

the person in question was a heavy set individual who
was walking with a ponderous gait and it would only
be a matter of minutes before joe caught up with him
or her.

good, thought joe, perhaps this person will prove to
be friendly and will give me some useful information
or even advice about what to expect in the city.

joe came up behind the person, who was wearing a
heavy gray cloak, even though the weather was on
the warm side, and a tall black hat. like a magician?
joe wondered, as he recalled seeing a few television
shows about magicians although they had not much

interested him, not as much as shows about bigfoot or serial killers or homicide detectives.

joe drew abreast of the person, and wished it a cheerful good morning.

the person turned its face - a long sad oval face - to joe and the first thing joe noticed was a huge purple clown nose in the middle of it.

a clown! joe knew that clowns existed but had never given them much thought, let alone considered becoming one himself.

in fact he did not have a very clear idea of what clowns did, if anything.

"good morning to yourself," the clown-faced personage returned joe's greeting, in a deep rumbling voice, giving joe confidence that the person was, as he had suspected, male.

"a fine morning," joe offered in an attempt to continue the conversation.

"some might think so," replied the clown, "some might think so." joe noticed for the first time that the clown was carrying a heavy stick in his hand, which joe had not noticed as it had been concealed by the clown's bulk, and by his cape.

the clown shook his stick at joe, though not in a threatening manner. "i percieve, young man, that you have the cheerful countenance of one whose experience of the world is none the most comprehensive."

"that is true, sir. in fact i have just been released into the world this morning."

"i see. you have a confident enough air. would it be presumptuous to ask what your plans, if any, are, as you proceed along the high road into the great metropolis?"

"well,sir " joe replied, encouraged by the clown's show of polite interest ," i have not given the matter as much thought as perhaps i might . i have thought of perhaps becoming a billionaire, or a movie director, or a lone wolf dispensing solitary justice, as i know that these are some of the occupations available to humans in the modern world. "

the clown laughed. "that is all very well, young man, but these occupations, as you cal them, do not account for a very large proportion of the world's daily endeavors. i did not have a head for figures, but i know that persons engaging in them amount to very much less than 1 percent of the world's population."

"i am not very good at mathematics myself," joe admitted. "but perhaps i could settle for being a homicide detective, and matching wits with serial killers."

"ha ha! so you would rather be a homicide detective and not a serial killer yourself, eh?"

"oh no, sir! as much as i might enjoy matching wits with homicide detectives, i have an abhorrence of violence, and would not wish to inflict any harm on my fellow creatures."

"worthy sentiments. we can only hope that you hold to them as you penetrate more deeply into this sadly compromised and unforgiving world."

"what about yourself, sir? are you a clown? or perhaps a magician? as you seem to exhibit some of the outward signs of both those time honored identities."

"i am both a clown and a magician, my young friend, as well as a poet, a dreamer, a visionary, and the architect of a better future for all living things."

joe's eyes widened. "i see," he said.

"you do not seem impressed."

"oh but sir, i am, i am indeed!" joe protested.

"my name is magnus, by the way," the clown-poet-visionary continued, fixing joe with his dark gaze, but not breaking stride as he did so.

"my name is joe, and i am pleased to meet you."

4. cupcakes, religion, and detectives

joe continued along the road with his new acquaintance magnus.

they did not encounter any other foot travelers.

a few vehicles - trucks, buses, and motorcycles - passed them, all headed into the city.

joe began to feel hungry, and he took one of teresa's chocolate cupcakes out of his pocket.

he felt that it would only be polite to offer the other one in his pocket to magnus, and he did so.

magnus regarded the proferred cupcake a bit dubiously but accepted it. "why thank you, young man, that is very kind of you. are you sure you can spare it, and will not suffer any pangs of hunger because of your generosiry?"

"oh no, sir," joe laughed. "i am sure civilization has progressed to the point where no one need suffer pangs of hunger, except perhaps in pursuit of some religious ideal."

magnus had started to put the cupcake in his mouth but stopped. "hmm. so you are an expert on religion, are you?'"

joe blushed a little. "no, sir, far from it, i am sorry to say. of course we had a little library in our home with copies of the basic texts of all the major religions - buddhism, christianity, judaism, islam, marxism, darwinism and so forth - as required of mother to be granted a license to procreate - but i am afraid i did not peruse it as assiduously as i might."

"i see, " magnus replied. "well, nothing to be ashamed of there. few in this ignorant age avail themselves of the opportunities for knowledge so dutifully provided by such authority as prevails in these degenerate and unredeemed times - but, you are young yet, and who knows..." the sage seemed to lose his train of thought, and took a bite of the chocolate cupcake.

"that is true, sir, who knows?" joe agreed.

"i say, this is quite tasty." magnus , having bitten off and swallowed half the cupcake, flourished the remaining half at joe. "did you make it yourself? you should sell them, if you do., make a bundle."

"i did not bake it myself, my sister did," joe admitted. "i was never much for cooking or baking, almost of my experience in day to day life consisted of taking care of animals, particularly pigs, with whom i enjoyed a natural rapport."

"mmm," magnus replied, with his mouth full of the other half of the cupcake.

"what exactly did you mean by a bundle, sir, when you spoke of the commercial possibilities of my sister's cupcakes? the recipe for them has mutated through several generations of smith females. by a bundle do you mean a billion dollars? because i would very much like to be a billionaire."

"no, no, nothing like that." magnus brushed a few cupcake crumbs off his jaw. "but a person might survive selling a few on the street corner, that is all i meant."

"oh."

"ha, ha! do not make such a long face. survival is not to be sneezed at, in these perilous times. why i, myself, an accredited poet and sage of the twelfth degree, am quite happy to survive." magnus sighed. "yes, happy just to survive."

joe did not care for the direction the conversation was taking, and changed the subject.

"do you know, sir, how i would go about becoming a homicide detective? al things considered, i think that is the path i would like to pursue in the great city, at least at first."

"why, i have never given the matter much thought. i suppose you could inquire at any police station, of which there are no lack in this city or in any city. i would guess you would have to start out as an

ordinary patrolman, unless you had some sort of
extraordinary qualifications."

"but surely, sir, you must know some homicide
detectives?" joe persisted.

"why no, i do not believe i have ever made the
personal acquaintance of one."

"you haven't?"

joe was shocked. how could a person reach an
advanced age living in a large city and not know a
single homicide detective?

he wondered if he should ask the sage if he knew any
trained deadly assassins, or any vampire hunters?

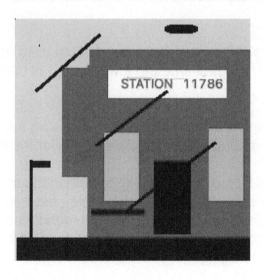

5. in sight of the city

joe and magnus rounded a bend in the road and joe beheld for the first time the towers and tall buildings of the city.

a few more vehicles passed them heading into the city, and a couple of helicopters flew over their heads.

so far joe was a little bit disappointed in his travels. he had thought to meet more people , but had only encountered magnus, who, though friendly enough, had not been particularly helpful, had in fact been a little discouraging.

suddenly joe was hungry. the wondered if he should take another of teresa's cupcakes out of his gag, or one of the sandwiches he had made that morning.

but it was not even noon! he supposed the walking had made him hungry. but he decided not to show weakness and he left the cupcakes and sandwiches alone.

magnus's negative reaction to joe's questions about becoming a homicide detective had made him hesitant to make any other enquires about employment in the city.

but as he was wondering if he should reopen the subject, they came to the outskirts of the city, and a large park, with trees, park benches, and many signs for buses and other transportation.

magnus, who had slowed down a bit - joe had politely kept pace with him - plopped down on the first empty park bench, with a somewhat dramatic sigh.

"well, young man, it has been a pleasure talking to you, but i need to rest my ancient carcass, so i will leave you to speed up your pace as you make your way in - " magnus hesitated. "as you make your way."

"why, it has been a pleasure for me too, sir," joe replied. "perhaps we shall meet again." joe could not imagine that the city was so big that he would not cross the sage's path again, perhaps many times.

"that may well be," magnus replied. "one never knows."

"perhaps, sir, as you are a clown and a magician and so forth, you will be performing in some capacity soon. maybe i will see you then."

if magnus was surprised by joe's interest - or his politeness in feigning interest - he did not show it.

"why, as a matter of fact, i happen to have a schedule here -" he produced some cards from beneath his cape and offered two of them to joe. "please - take one. take two - give one to some other curious wanderer through life's thorny path."

"thank you, sir." joe glanced at one of the cards. it consisted of a series of dates, with the venues for each in small print, beneath a blurry photo of a somewhat younger magnus, and the motto "architect of a new world."

magnus nodded with a somewhat wistful smile, and joe took his leave of him.

joe decided to find a park bench of his own, where he could eat one of sandwiches - because by now he was decidedly hungry - and consider his prospects.

it occurred to him that he had never actually asked magnus what he had in mind when he spoke of being the "architect" of some future world.

that was rude of me, thought joe, as he took a seat on a bench beneath a wide and shady elm.

as he unwrapped his sandwich, he resolved to attempt to be more courteous in the future.

6. johnny

"that's a tasty looking sandwich, bro. did you make it yourself?"

joe had been so intent on devouring his sandwich that he had not noticed that another person had seated himself on the bench beside him.

hastily swallowing the bit of unmasticated food in his mouth, he turned and saw a young man of about his own age, small and thin and wearing plain white clothing - like a nurse or hospital orderly? - and staring at him with small dark eyes like he was looking into the final conflagration of time and space.

joe welcomed all human contact, and replied, "yes, i did as a matter of fact. i had always been taught that preparing one's own food was a useful way of conserving energy and cutting the daily cost of living."

joe wondered as he spoke if he should offer the young man one of his other sandwiches, but some obscure instinct - or unconscious calculation that he did not have an infinite number of sandwiches to distribute - held him back.

he did not offer the young man one of teresa's cupcakes either.

"you *had* been taught," the young man was saying, "does that mean you are not being taught any more?"

"that is an interesting point," joe responded politely, although he actually thought the question was pretty stupid. "i had not thought of it in quite that way before. my name is joe smith by the way, what is yours?'

"johnny jones."

"i am pleased to meet you, johnny."

"you must be easily pleased. ha ha, just kidding. i
am pleased to meet you too, joe." johnny replied, but
without relaxing his somewhat menacing stare.

"you're a rube, aren't you, joe?" johnny continued.
"fresh from the country."

"oh no, " said joe. "i was always led to believe that i
was not from either the country or the city, but just in
between."

"oh? well just between you and me , joe, i think most
people would put you down as a complete yokei, a
hick from hicksville, and a good old-fashioned
plowboy. not that there is anything wrong with any of
those things." and for the first time johnny's face
showed a trace of a smile.

"well," said joe, "there was someplace called the country, which was in the opposite direction from the city, and i flipped a coin and decided to come here to the city, and here i am."

"yes, i see that you are here," said johnny. "and my question to you is, now that you are here, where are you , and where do you go from here?"

 joe was not in the least surprised or displeased at such questions from a complete stranger , had in fact been expecting them, and he began to tell his new acquaintance, as he had told magnus, his thoughts on becoming a homicide detective or lone avenger, his experiences with the pigs and other creatures, and various other things that popped into his head as he talked.

johnny listened with what joe took to be polite intetest.

suddenly a tremendous noise arose from behind the trees surrounding the park. a noise which joe first thought might be a bomb, but then recognized as loud music.

johnny turned toward the trees. "the meeting has begun," he told joe.

7. behind the trees

"what meeting?" asked joe.

"come along, rube," said johnny, "and maybe you might be enlightened, or at least learn something."

johnny got up from the park bench and headed toward the trees, and after a moment's hesitation joe put what was left of his sandwich - about one quarter of it - into his pocket and followed him.

they went down a short dirt road between some trees and came out into a park...

where a crowd of more people than joe had ever seen in his life were gathered around a bandstand. some were seated on concrete seats in a sunken circular auditorium but many more were sitting or standing in the grass in a wider circle.

the band was really loud and playing some kind of
music. the music was really loud and sounded like
almost all music did to joe - just a lot of noise.

a large woman in a white suit - a better cut version of
the white clothes johnny jones was wearing - was
standing in front of a microphone about ten feet in
front of the band. there was a banner above her head
but they were too far away for joe to read it.

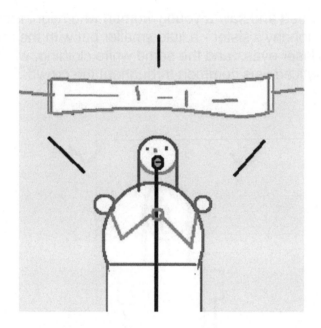

"is she going to sing?" joe asked johnny. joe did not
mind singing quite so much as he minded music
played on instruments. (he particularly disliked music
played on any kind of horns. pianos and guitars he
could almost enjoy sometimes.)

johnny laughed. "no, rube, she is not going to sing. that is alice - alice cartwright devine herself - the savior of the world."

"oh." joe had never heard of alice cartwright devine but did not say so.

"who's your friend?" came a voice behind joe and johnny.

joe turned and saw a young woman who might have been johnny's sister - a little smaller but with the same dark laser eyes. and the same white clothing, which joe noticed was common throughout the crowd.

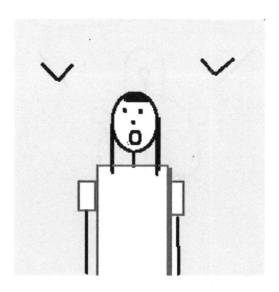

in response to the girl's question, johnny turned to joe. "what did you say your name was?" he asked.

"joe. joe smith."

"don't mind him," said the girl to joe. "that's just the way he is. he probably calls you slim or hoss or bucky or something like that, right?"

"rube," joe admitted.

"that's even worse," said the girl. "my name is mary brown. i am pleased to meet you. i see you are not wearing white. is this your first time hearing alice speak?"

"yes, it is," joe admitted. "in fact i never heard of her before, and do not have any idea what she is going to talk about."

"i told you he was a rube," said johnny.

"well, he is not ashamed to admit his ignorance, which is a most admirable way to be, and which some people could take example from."

joe was wondering what, if anything to reply, when the music suddenly stopped.

alice cartwright devine said "testing" into the microphone and the word carried loudly over the crowd and the crowd applauded.

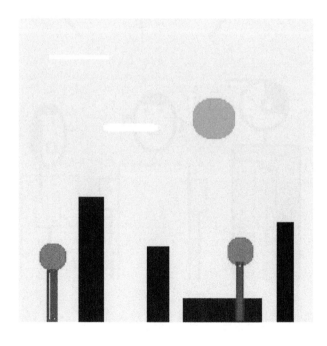

8. alice

"al-ice! al-ice! al-ice!" the crowd began chanting.

joe's new friends johnny and mary clapped their
hands and joined the chant, but joe thought there was
something not entirely convincing about their
enthusiasm.

of course joe was too polite to say so.

the chanting and clapping died down, and alice
cartwright devine began speaking.

"thank you all and good evening," she began, " i have
a very important announcement to make, so please
listen carefully."

the crowd grew quiet.

"as you know, we embarked on this great adventure - of starting a new religion which would transform the world and human consciousness - a little over two years ago."

some scattered applause in the crowd.

"we were particularly inspired to do so by the need to counteract the insidious teachings and preachings of the sworn enemy of humankind and the earth, mister william jennings bryan."

"boo! boo! boo! down with bryan!" some of the crowd chanted, a little more loudly, joe thought, than they had cherred alice herself."

"and it has been a long, wonderful two years that we have worked and prayed together and i thank you with all my heart."

joe still had no idea what she was talking about, but did not say so to johnny and mary.

"starting a new religion," alice continued, "is not for the faint of heart."

"true that!" a few members of the crowd shouted.

"but i have come to the conclusion" said alice, "that i no longer have what it takes to try to change the hearts of people raised on countless millennia of lies and falsehoods, so i have decided to step down from my position as head of the path to tomorrow, and to take up a new life. i wish you all the best, and i hope that you respect my decision and will not be too disappointed. anyone who wishes to continue the ministry of the path to tomorrow is of course free and more than welcome to do so."

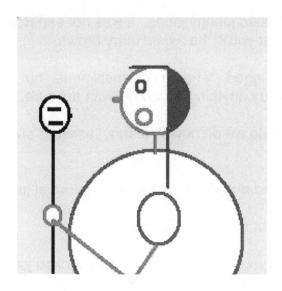

"no! no!" cried a few feeble voices from the crowd, which had already begun to drift away,

"it won't be the same without you, alice!" a lonely voice floated over the crowd.

and another, even lonelier voice added, "you were the path to tomorrow!"

"in conclusion," said alice, "i would like it thank my two most devoted followers, johnny jones and mary brown, for all their efforts. the path to tomorrow would never have gotten past the first ten feet without them. now please enjoy this last stirring rendition of "the road to the road is the road to the road" by the path to tomorrow brass band. thank you."

alice stepped away from the microphone. most of the crowd had already dispersed.

"damn!" said johnny jones. "i was not expecting that. how about you?" he asked mary brown.

mary shrugged. "i had a few suspicions. but i didn't want to say anything because i was not sure."

"so what do we do now?" johnny asked. "any ideas?"

johnny and mary both turned and looked at joe.

"how about this guy?" asked mary.

"what do you say, big guy?" johnny looked joe in the eye. "how would you like to start a new religion, a brand new religion?"

"um - it is not something i ever thought about ," said joe.

"i know, i know," said johnny ,"you want to be a homicide detective or a lone avenger."

"those things are not as easy to become as you might think," mary told joe. "there is a lot of competiton - a lot of competition."

joe hesitated. he did not want to hurt their feelings.

"i tell you what," said johnny. "why don't you come home with us tonight, and we will talk about it in the morning?"

joe had begun to wonder where he was going to sleep that night, so he said, "all right."

9. a change in plans

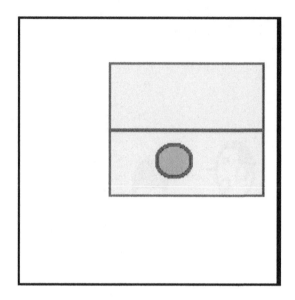

joe woke up. it took him a few seconds to remember where he was.

he was on the couch in johnny's and mary's apartment, and not back home in the barracks room he had shared with five of his brothers.

joe could see the sun shining through the little window in the breakfast nook where johnny and mary were sipping coffee in paper cups and muttering to each other.

mary noticed that joe was awake and said good morning to him. johnny just nodded in joe's direction.

"good morning," joe answered.

"want some breakfast?" mary asked.

"yes, i would, thank you."

mary pointed to a white paper bag on a counter behind her. "help yourself."

joe picked up the bag and saw it had a mcdonalds logo in it. he looked inside and it contained a couple of egg mcmuffins.

"can i have them both?" joe asked hesitantly.

"i see you are a growing boy with a big appetite," mary answered. "yeah, you can have both of them. and there is coffee over there if want some."

"thank you." joe poured some thick black coffee from the pot on the counter into a paper cup and sat down with it and the bag of egg mcmuffins.

although he had eaten at mcdonalds on special occasions, joe was used to getting up in the morning and having big walloping helpings of powdered eggs and quaker oats - washed down with yoo-hoo chocolate drink - before going out and tending to his pigs.

right now, he missed the pigs but did not say so to johnny and mary.

he wondered what this new day held in store for him.

joe felt mary's eyes on him. johnny looked asleep in his chair.

"um -" joe began, "did you say something last night about starting a new religion?"

"we are going to put that on hold," johnny answered immediately.

"yes," mary added. "we decided to do something different, at least for now. instead of starting a new religion, we are going to rob a bank."

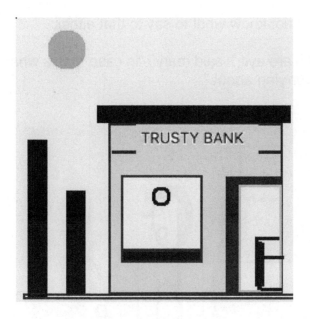

"oh." joe did not know what else to say.

"would you care to join us?" johnny asked.

"well - i don't know," said joe. "it is not something i ever thought of before."

"last nght you had never thought of starting a new religion before, but you were willing to go along with that," mary pointed out.

43

"yes, but - aren't they two kind of different things?'
joe asked.

"the same quality of forthright innocence you have
which would have been helpful in starting a religion
can also be put to good use in robbing a bank," said
johnny.

joe did not know what to say to that either.

"banks are evil," said mary. "in case that is what you
are worrying about."

"yes, i know," said joe.

"and besides," said johnny, "we might rob a casino
instead of a bank, and they are even more evil."

joe took a bite of one of the egg mcmuffins.

10. the casino

after some discussion, johnny and mary decided to
hold up a casino.

joe was down to his last few dollars of savings,
because he decided to go along with johnny and mary
for at least another day, because they had been nice
enough to let him sleep on their couch.

the casino was on the other side of town.

they took the bus. the only other person on the bus
besides the driver was an old man reading the bible,
who did not look up at joe, johnny, and mary.

the old man's lips moved as he read the bible. joe
thought he looked kind of familiar, not like someone
he had ever actually known, but like se actor he had
seen on tv.

when they got to the casino, night had completely
fallen, and the street was dark.

joe was not exactly disappointed, but a little surprised
at how small and shabby the "casino" was.

from the outside, it looked something like a
laundromat. through the thick glass windows, he
could see men and a few women sitting around round
tables. many of the men wore hats.

a barely readable sign in the window said - poker -
pan - pai gow- california blackjack.

joe had heard of poker and blackjack. he did not
know what "california blackjack" was and had never
heard of pan or pai gow,

"what a dump," said mary. "you sure this is the right place?"

"it's the right address," said johnny. "i heard it was not too flashy. but i wasn't expecting to be quite like this."

"it looks like mostly poker," said mary.

"we're here, we might as well check it out, " said johnny. he looked at joe. "you know how to play poker?"

"um - i'm not sure."

"what do you know about poker?"

"i know a royal flush is the best hand."

"you need to know a little more than that. i will check the place out, you two wait here."

"it's cold out!" mary protested.

"there was a little dunkin donuts back at the bus stop. you can wait for me there."

"all right."

joe and mary watched johnny enter the "casino". then they went around the corner and headed for the dunkin donuts.

they passed a dark doorway with a hulking figure standing in it. joe thought it looked like magnus but the figure did not call to him and they passed it by.

11. the boomer

johnny pushed open the door of the casino and walked in.

nobody at the tables looked up at him.

a guy with an apron was collecting at one of the tables and he glanced up at johnny when he finished and started toward another table.

"be right with you," the man with the apron said. he wore a white shirt and a black tie, in the classic style.

johnny looked around. there were ten tables, but games going on at only three. one of the tables, in a corner, seemed to have no house dealer. but the man with the apron went over and collected from the players, so johnny figured it was a real game.

"so - what can i do for you?" the man asked johnny when he was finished collecting.

"what have you got?"

"three and six. five and ten. three seats open in the five and ten. two in the three and six."

"what's that over there?" johnny pointed to the table with no dealer.

"draw poker."

"draw poker! what is it, the last one on earth?"

"you interested?"

"hell no, just curious. " johnny looked over at the table. there were five players, all old men, and they did not look at all like high rollers. "what kind of money do they play for?"

"it depends. depends on who's playing. we keep it going for the boomer. the boomer likes to play it sometimes."

whoever he might be, thought johnny. "i'll take the five and ten," he told the floorman.

"hundred buy-in. and i just collected. two every hour."

that's cheap enough, johnny did not say out loud. "no problem." he said.

"you want down for ten and twenty, if i can get it going?"

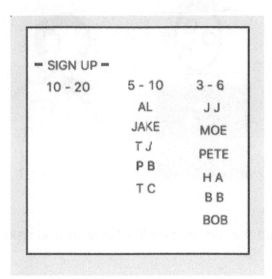

sure, why not?"

johnny heard a big laugh behind him. he turned and saw magnus.

"what are you doing running around loose?'" magnus asked johnny. "isn't there any law in this town?"

"i could ask you the same," was the best johnny could come up with.

"you know this bum?" the floorman asked johnny.

"i guess i do."

"you want the five and ten?", the floorman asked magnus.

"indeed. and put me up for anything bigger."

there were two empty seats together at the five and ten table and johnny and magnus took them and the floorman began counting out chips for them.

"what's your name?' the floorman asked johnny, "so i can put you down for the ten and twenty?"

"j j"

"we already got a j j here."

"jones."

"all right, mr jones."

"what's your name?" johnny asked with a smile.

"albert."

"you own this place?"

"no, i just work here. why do you ask?"

"just curious."

"you two guys want to kill it, or wait?" the dealer, a large blonde woman, asked johnny and magnus.

magnus tossed some chips in the center of the table, and johnny did the same.

"you a regular here?" johnny asked magnus as the cards were being dealt.

"i come and go. you know how it is."

"right."

johnny looked at his cards. the three of diamonds and the nine of clubs.

12. a pair of fours

johnny quickly discovered that if the cops raided the joint they wouldn't arrest anybody in the five and ten game for gambling.

"it seems a little slow here," he observed to magnus. "i thought it would are a little livelier."

"that's because the boomer isn't here, " magnus answered, as he glanced at the two cards he had just been dealt and threw them away.

johnny looked at a pair of fours, and decided against his better judgment to play them.

"that's right," the dealer, whose name tag identified her as alexis, agreed. "if the boomer was here, you'd see something."

two of the other players laughed appreciatively at this remark, as if to say, "yeah, that boomer, he's something all right."

only the big blind, a woman who looked like a bag lady, stayed in against johnny.

the flop was ace king nine, three different suits,.

"it's on you, danny," the dealer told the bag lady looking woman, and she bet five.

johnny called, just to show the other players he would play once in a while.

"so this boomer," said johnny. "i guess they build the games around him when he comes in?"

"the whole place is built around him, " said alexis the dealer. "when he comes in."

"but he isn't been in in a while," said another player. "that is why the place is so dead."

the dealer turned over a four and danny bet ten and johnny raised another ten and danny called.

the last card in the flop was an ace. danny bet ten and johnny raised ten and danny raised another ten.

johnny called and danny showed a pair of kings giving her kings full to johnny's fours full.

"that is enough for me," said johnny. he glanced over at magnus.

magnus understood that johnny wanted to talk to him, so he said, "me too," and they both got up and headed for the door.

as they exited, a distinguished looking gray haired man in a three piece suit passed them on his way in. the man glanced at magnus and nodded but neither of them spoke.

johnny looked back at the man. "i don't suppose that was the boomer."

magnus laughed. "no, that wasn't the boomer."

it had gotten colder outside and johnny shivered. "okay, so who is this boomer? anybody i want to get acquainted with?"

"that depends," said magnus.

13. blow this town

mary seemed distracted, staring out the window of the dunkin donuts and sipping her coffee and nibbling on an apple danish, as she and joe waited for johnny.

it occurred to joe that it was the first time he had ever been alone with a human female, except for his mother and his sisters.

of course they were not really "alone" as there were a few other people in the dunkin donuts, and a couple of people behind the counter.

suddenly mary looked over at joe, as if she was surprised he was there.

"what did you say your name was?" she asked joe.

"joe. joe smith."

"oh, yeah, right. and what is your purpose, joe? why did we pick you up?"

"something about starting a new religion?"

"oh yeah, right, how could i forget?"

joe laughed uneasily. "well, i don't know, i would have thought that starting a new religion was a little bit of a big deal. something that you would remember at least for a day." he smiled at mary who did not smile back. "but, hey what do i know?"

"what you don't know is johnny, who is always talking about starting new religions and all other kinds of new things."

"oh."

"and he usually ends up deciding to rob banks instead
- or mom and pop stores."

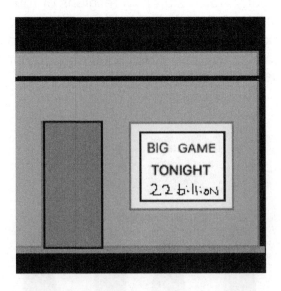

"oh. well - i was just trying to be helpful. i don't really
know much about new religions - or about robbing
banks either."

"what *do* you know, joe, if you don't mind my asking?"

"not much, i guess.":

mary laughed again, but in a more friendly way this
time. "that's all right, joe. nobody really knows
anything. that's why the world is the way it is. did you
ever stop and think about that?"

joe had absolutely no idea what mary was talking
about. "uh - no, not really/"

"look at this way. if anybody knew what was going on, people would just get up in the morning and they would know what they had to do and they would just do it. nobody would start new religions or rob convenience stores or write books or direct movies or sit around in cafes or donut shops arguing about stuff - they would just know what they had to do and they would just do it. make sense?"

"so do you want to start a new religion?" joe asked, just to be saying something.

mary leaned forward and looked joe in the eyes. "no, you know what i want to do?"

"what?"

"i want to start a whole new way of looking at the world - synthesizing and superseding all religions, all so-called science, all human perception, all human history. what do you think?"

"sounds like you must have some confidence in yourself." joe wondered if anyone in the donut shop was overhearing their conversation. he glanced around, but it did not seem that anybody was, or if they were, they were not interested.

"i can see why johnny picked you up," mary said. "you have a real innocent look about you, real polite, you don't look like you want to laugh in peoiple's faces or be somewhere else when people talk to you. the perfect face for starting a new religion - or a new way of looking at the world."

"it's just the way i am, i guess."

mary looked out the window at the night. "i tell you what, joe. why don't we blow this town? shake the dust of this hick town off our feet and head for the big city? just you and me, forget johnny."

"the big city?" joe was bewildered. "but i thought this was the big city! i mean - it is in the opposite way from the country, that is why i am here."

"ha ha! well, maybe it is not quite the country country, but it isn't a real city either. no, i was thinking of heading for a real city, like omaha or chicago or even vancouver or tokyo."

joe did not know what to answer.

"don't worry about johnny, if that is what you are thinking. we were just about to go our separate ways anyway, and he can take care of himself. up to a point, anyway. so are you with me ?"

"all right."

"that's the spirit. come on, let's get out of here before he gets back. we won't have to waste time saying good-byes. because - ." mary drained the last of her cup of coffee and brushed some donut crumbs off her pants - " i hate good-byes."

14. down to business

the first thing johnny noticed when he entered the
dunkin donuts was that mary and joe were gone.

he looked around just to make sure, but it was a small
place, and they were not there.

"looking for somebody?" magnus asked him.

"yeah, i was expecting a couple of friends here, but i
guess they got tired of waiting." johnny knew that
they had skipped out on him and he would probably
never see them again.

just as well, he thought, if he could get something
going with magnus.

"i'm a little short," magnus anounced as johnny headed for the counter.

"that's all right, get what you want, it's my treat."

"you are a true gentleman, sir, one of the last.," magnus smiled. "but i won't abuse your hospitality, at least not this time. a small black coffee, please, and a plain cruller," he told the young woman behind the counter.

johnny got a large black coffee with three sugars and a glazed donut and they took a seat in the corner as far ftom the other patrons as they could get. magnus could look out the window - and be seen by people passing by, but johnny could not.

johnny got down to business. "all right, tell me about this boomer character."

magnus laughed. "why the interest? surely you are not going back to playing cards full time? i have to say i was surprised to even see you at zack's."

"zack's? that was the name of the place?"

"you didn't know?"

"maybe, i don't remember. i just heard it was a place, you know?"

magnus just nodded.

"a place with some serious action. but it would seem that i was misinformed." johnny lowered his voice. "but between you and me, i was not so much interested in playing there. actually playing at the tables."

"ah." magnus dropped his voice too. "but that sort of activity, my friend, is even less remumerative these days than sitting at a table. as i am sure you know."

"yeah, i know, but what can you do?" johnny looked casually around., but nobody seemed to be paying them any attention. "but, back to serious business. any idea where my sources got the idea that this zack's was worth a look?"

"i can tell you exactly why. the boomer."

"ah, back to the boomer. who is he - the richest man in the world?"

"ha, ha, i don't know about that. he does have some money to spread around when he is in the mood. he's a man who attracts notice - a man who stirs people up. and wakes people up. surely you heard the undercurrents of awe when his name was mentioned."

johnny considered this. "like a preacher. a guy working a religion angle. welcome to the club."

magnus shook his head. "no, not really."

"no? all right, let's start over. do you really know anything about this character? i am not cross-examining you, i am just curious."

"well, let me think. what do i know about our friend the boomer? i have never really given him that much thought because i never saw him as providing any opportunities or myself."

"you surprise me, old buddy. you used to be a guy who looked at all the angles."

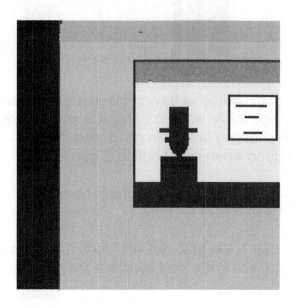

15. an invitation to dinner

"the maid we assigned to the staffords has informed
me that mr stafford is indisposed, and will not be
coming down to dinner."

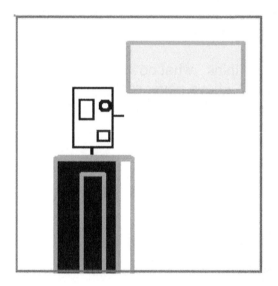

"on top of m santcerre having the same complaint.
what do you think, wallace? that it is something in the
air? the shooting has been good, and the air is
usually good when the shooting is good."

 "i really can't say, madame. shall i have cook
proceed with dinner for ten?"

"no, no, that is too few. not with such a guest as mr
mahmoud, you know how sensitive they can be about
trifles."

wallace nodded, indicating that he awaited mrs foster's command.

"i know it is tiresome, but you shall have to go out into the highways and byways and round up a couple of guests. it is short notice, but do what you can."

"yes, madame. and i will tell cook to proceed with dinner for twelve."

*

stone, mrs foster's chauffeur, pulled the old bentley - the family's oldest car, used for the most functional and last ceremonial purposes - off the driveway and on to the "highway and byway" in which he and wallace, the butler, were to find a pair of guests to complete the evening dinner party.

"what are we looking for, mr wallace?"

"the first people who come along, stone. the first people who come along.

"ha, ha. surely you have some more stringent requirements than that, mr wallace?"

"no, not at all." wallace looked out the window. "especially as it looks like rain. i really do not care to be driving around muddy roads in the bleak countryside all day to little purpose."

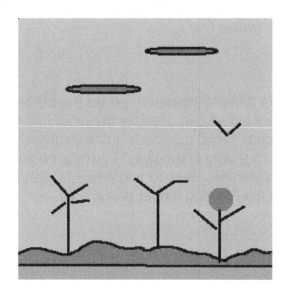

"so you have done the sort of thing before, have you?" stone asked. he was new to mrs foster's establishment.

"oh, yes, many times."

"and you have never found that the people you just pick up by the side of the road cause any - any embarrassment when they are introduced to the society of the likes of mrs foster and her distinguished guests - heads of state, the cream of society, and all that?"

"not at all."

stone laughed. "really? they never misbehave, or express any disgruntled proletarian or anti-establishment sentiments?"

"never. i have found that people, even the lowest of the low, are always quite properly in awe of their betters, and mind their manners quire nicely."

wallace and stone lapsed into silence, and continued to drive along. perhaps because of the threatening skies, the roads were deserted.

the rain began to fall.

stone was just about to head for the main highway and the roads into the city when they saw a young man and a young woman trudging along ahead of them.

mary heard the bentley behind them before joe did, and moved a bit off the road, so as not to get splashed by the rainwater.

but the bentley stopped. wallace rolled the window down and explained his and stone's mission.

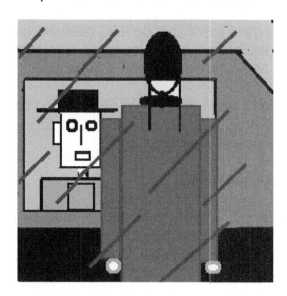

mary listened attentively, when wallace was finished,
she asked, "so we get some free food?"

"yes, miss, and quite a bit of it, if that is your fancy.
one thing about mrs foster, she is no cheeseparer.
and expects no great show of gratitude, either. you
will not be required to sing for your supper."

"sounds good." mary nodded to joe.

"the rear door is unlocked," wallace told them, and
they both got in the car.

wallace noticed that joe had not said a word, but had
let mary do all the talking.

16. angeline

angeiline watched through the rain streaked windows
as mr mahmoud and his private secretary arrived.
she had begged off easily enough from being in the
greeting party, and her mother had assured her that
neither mr mahmoud nor the secretary would give a
moment's thought to her, whether she was there or
not.

angeline watched as mr mahmoud and the secretary
and two other men - bodyguards? - got out of mr
mahmoud's heavy looking - bulletproof? - car. she
thought it quite vulgar though just a bit thrilling that the
two men might be carrying guns under their long
black coats.

"what do you think the best place to be sure of avoiding these fellows?" she asked mademoiselle feval, the governess.

"either the blue room or the library," replied mademoiselle. "the blue room is the more out of the way, but it seems unlikely that any would seek the library - even assuming that their duties would allow them to seek anything."

"the library it is, then, " said angeline, turning from the window.

just then rogers, the under-butler, appeared. "i just installed a couple of guests in the library, miss. a couple of emergency guests that mr wallace hastily recruited, because two others had begged off from dinner."

angeline shrugged. "thank you, rogers. but in that case i shall be curious to meet them. i do not suppose they are carrying guns on their persons?"

"i assume they are not, miss," rogers replied with a smile.

*

joe and mary looked up when angeline and mademoiselle feval entered the library.   they were both seated in deep armchairs, reading books they had found on the shelves.

joe was reading "the adventures of philip", by wlliam makepeace thackeay, and mary was reading volume 14 of professor harrison's history of world religions.

angeline smiled at them as pleasantly as she was able. "i hope you are quite comfortable."

"yes we are, thank you," mary replied evenly, lowering her book. "mr wallace told us we could stay here until dinner."

"oh, i do not doubt that," angeline assured mary. "i do not question your being here." she took a seat in a chair close to mary's. "it is a dreary day, isn't it? otherwise we might go outside and play a little croquet, or badminton."

"i have never played either of those games," said mary, "no doubt they have their estimable qualities."

"oh, they are just something to do, when one had to do something, as one is expected to do most of the time. look here, that is quite a tome you have selected there. are you really as interested as all that in the history of religion?"

"yes, i am, " mary replied.

"and why is that, if i may ask?" angeline persisted.
"are you a devotee of any established religion
yourself".

"no, i was thinking of starting my own religion."

"oh. you know, that seems to be all the rage these
days. we have had quite a few guests lately who
have expressed the same inclination. in fact, we
might have some right now who do."

"that is very interesting," mary replied with a polite
smile.

"perhaps you could get together with them and compare notes," observed mademoiselle feval.

"perhaps they could," angeline agreed. "if most of them were not so terribly busy rearranging the map of the world." she glanced at mary. "we have some frightfully important guests, you know, whom you shall see at dinner. such as mr mahmoud. you know who mr mahmoud is. of course."

"of course," mary answered. "i have seen him many times - on television."

"and what opinion, if any, have you formed of him?" asked mademoiselle feval.

17. boys night out

"it's a nice clear night, dear. i think i will go for a little walk."

"so soon? did you not go for one just a few nights ago?"

"no, it was more than two weeks ago, i just checked my diary. i can show it to you if you like."

"oh no, i believe you. but i think it is supposed to be rather chilly out."

"i will bundle up. i will wear that nice scarf you bought me for my birthday. it will be the perfect occasion for it."

"very well then. have a good time. i know how much you enjoy your nights out with the boys, as you call them."

"thank you, dear. i hope you have a nice pleasant evening yourself."

ernestine watched as charles collected his hat, scarf, cap, and umbrella and closed the door behind him.

and then waited a minute more until she heard the elevator arrive. the elevator made almost no noise, but she had exceptional hearing.

and then she went to the window and watched as charles emerged on to the sidewalk, exchanged a few words with the doorperson, and then headed down the street toward the lit up shops and restaurants.

when he was gone from view, ernestine took out her phone and punched in a number she was careful not to have on speed dial.

jeffrey answered right away, as he almost always did.

"jeffrey? it's ernestine. charles has gone out for the evening. if you are free and would like to come over. "

"why yes, that's sounds jolly. i have a few little things to attend to, but then i shall be right over."

"until then,"

*

the berkeley was one of the smallest banks still in existence, but was open - to those it was open to - twenty-four hours a day.

its office was completely unmarked and located above
a sushi shop and a baseball card collectors shop,
both of which were closed for the night when charles
arrived.

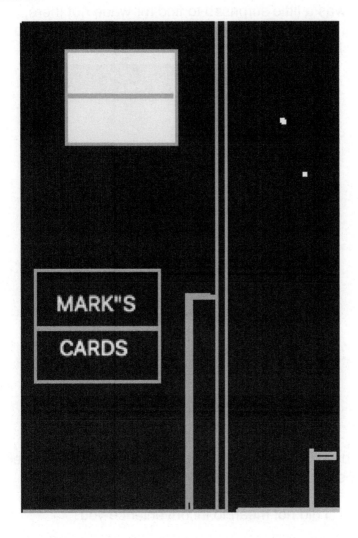

charles rang the banks unmarked bell and was
buzzed into the narrow staircase between the two
shops. he climbed the stairs in the dark and opened
the office door.

he was a little surprised to find mr wade not there,
and ms folger there in his place, seated at mr wade's
desk.

"a bit short notice this time, mr beaugard," ms folger
greeted him with a smile.

"oh? i did not mean to inconvenience you."

"not at all, not all, we are open twenty-four hours after all." ms folger continued to smile her little cat faced smile.

"i don't like to give my wife too much notice. not that she is likely to have me followed. mr wade agreed that it was a good policy.
"mr wade has been moved to another office. you will be dealing with me from now on, mr beaugard."

"oh. i see." charles was taken aback but tried not to show it.

"i tell you what," ms folger went on, "why don't you drop by some time tomorrow. says around two o'clock? we can discuss how we can best go forward."

"will there be any significant changes? " charles
asked, keeping his voice steady.

"i don't foresee any. but we will discuss it tomorrow."
ms folger reached into the desk drawer and began
taking out packets of money. "for tonight, just go on
about your business as usual."
"i will try," charles smiled, and began putting the
packets of money into the pockets of his overcoat.

"a bit chilly outside," ms folger observed.

"yes, it is."

18. a good thing

charles had a good thing going, one that kept him in pocket money and one that he wanted to keep going.

and one that he did not want ernestine to know about, although he did not know that it would really change anything if she did. but you never knew with ernestine.

when he had first taken the assignments from mr wade and begun his "boys nights out" he had thought ernestine might have him followed, but as time went on it became apparent that she did not.

no doubt being content with her own nights out with jeremy and gerard and peggy and her other friends.

but now this! charles could only wait and see if and how mr wade's departure - was it permanent? - would affect him.

it had all begun about a year ago when good old larry andrews had sent him around to mr wade.

mr wade had apparently liked what he saw in charles as being just the man he wanted because he had made his proposal and they had come to an agreement before charles had finished three drinks.

basically, charles went to the bank's offices at regular intervals and received large packs of cash. he was never told, and never asked, if the bills were "counterfeit" or not, and charles's understanding was that such a definition did not really mean much in the new world.

in any case, the "berkeley bank" whoever or
whatever it was and whoever was behind it, wanted
the bills circulated for their own purposes and gave
charles a small remuneration - in separate bills - to
spend them quickly and freely in places like race
tracks, casinos, betting parlors, and card rooms. i e, in
places where he did not have to go to much trouble
of establishing any identity beyond a nickname.
massage parlors, houses of ill repute, and even bars
were all right too, but not as much money could be
disposed of as quickly, and besides, charles preferred
the various gambling establishments.

in some of them he was "c b", in others "mr white" or
"chuckie" or "the boomer".

now, still slightly disoriented by the change at the
bank form mr wade to ms folger, he decided to head
for his favorite spot - zack's card room on the lower
north side.

as he passed the little dunkin donuts a couple of blocks from zack's he saw a familiar face from zack's - an old fashioned con man type who called himself professor - or was it doctor? - magnus.
a fellow charles found rather tiresome, but whose acquaintance he rather attempted to cultivate, out of an obscure feeling that he might someday be of use to him.

in case he, charles, might someday have to find a new identity and a new life, as was sadly so often the case in this chaotic modern world.

charles started to raise his hand to wave at magnus but just as he did magnus turned and spoke to someone out of charles's view.

19. a sudden inspiration

charles entered the dunkin donuts. magnus recognized him immediately and waved him over.

"boomer, old buddy, where have you been?" magnus pumped charles's hand. "i was just thinking about you."

"really? that's very flattering." charles disengaged his hand and sat down across from magnus and johnny. why had he come in here? he already regretted it. he did not really have anything to say to magnus, and would have preferred to be by himself thinking about his possibly changed circumstances.

magnus did not bother to introduce johnny, and
charles did not much like johnny's looks. he thought
he looked like a cheap two-bit grifter.

charles felt johnny's eyes on him. he turned to him
and gave him his most charming smile. "hello, there."

"hello, yourself," johnny answered evenly.

"oh, have you two gentlemen met?" magnus asked
innocently.

"i don't think so, " said johnny.

"boomer, this is j j, he used to be a regular at the
alligator club, over on the west side. j j, this the
boomer, that you might have heard people talking
about him back at zack's. we were at zack's last
night, " magnus told charles, "and were thinking of
heading over there now."

"how was the action there last night?" charles asked.

"pretty slow."

"hi see." suddenly charles did not want to go to zack's, or any place else. he wanted to get away somewhere and ponder his fate, speculate on the implications of his recent encounter with ms folger...

and then it hit him.

a plan formed in his mind, almost complete. magnus, with his flow of talk even if he had nothing else... and this punk, who looked mean enough even if he turned out to be not very bright... they were all he needed.

"say," charles said to magnus and johnny, with the air of a man who had just had a sudden inspiration, which in fact he had, "how would you two fellows like to make a few dollars?"

neither of them looked either surprised or particularly enthusiastic.

"i'll listen to anything." magnus told charles. "what's on your mind?"

"i'm not going anywhere," johnny added. "what have you got?"

charles looked around the dunkin donuts. "can we talk in here?"

"that's up to you," magnus told him.

"i know a place we can go - a little more private."

20. tarts

jeremy leaned back contentedly after finishing the
plate of cream tarts ernestine had whipped up for him.

"those were delightful, my dear, " he assured
ernestine.

"thank you."

"tell me, does charles never suspect you are making
these wonderful confections? surely, they must leave
some trace, in the air, or on the kitchen counter, or
somewhere?"

"oh, i am sure he does. but either he does not care -
that is the most likely explanation - or he just assumes
i eat them all myself."

"ah. and that you do not save any for him, does that
not bother him?"

"no, he is more of a cheeseburger and onion ring
person."

"how disgusting. a strange fellow, charles. i under
how he lives with himself, or how he continues to jog
along."

"the same way he always has. but enough about
charles, what about you? how are you getting along
in the great world since i last saw you?"

"oh, splendidly, splendidly. rising like a glob of
burning lava in a volcano. no one has a bad word to
say to me."

ernestine laughed. "a bad word *to* you? how about anything bad *about* you?"

"well, one never knows about that. i have not heard anything, that is best one can hope for, eh?"

"and have you been able to turn all this splendid rising and good words to any solid account?"

"why," jeremy replied carefully, "one has to observe certain proprieties, and not strike too quickly in these matters. let one's good fortune be so taken for granted that trading on it is not even noticed. i am sure you understand."

"of course, of course. and how is your charming wife?"

"moving from triumph to triumph."

"good. we wouldn't want her to miss out on the fun."

"yes," jeremy sighed. "everything would be perfect, if only the diplomatic situation were not quite so volatile."

"not so volatile? but don't you want it to be volatile? have you not made your whole career by being always a member of the war party?"

"of course, but always within limits."

"well, whatever. that is enough of that. i didn't think you came here to talk shop." ernestine leaned back and looked around the room. "come now, relax. is there anything else i can get you?"

"a plate of jelly tarts would be nice. and some more of this delightful tea to wash it down."

"coming right up."

ernestine got up from the sofa. as she did, the
doorbell rang.

whoever can that be, she wondered.

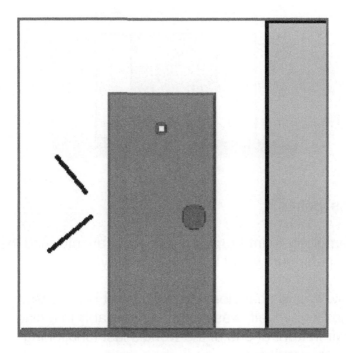

21. mr mahmoud

"yes, peters?"

"i am sorry to interrupt, my lord, but i an informed that mr mahmoud would like a word with you."

"now?" lord chandler glanced over at his nephew, who like himself, was seated comfortably in a club chair in front of one of the world's last functioning marble fireplaces.

"apparently so, my lord."

"how strange. well, i can't very well refuse him. show him in."

peters left and reentered with an unsmiling mr
mahmoud, who was unaccompanied by aides,
servants, or bodyguards.

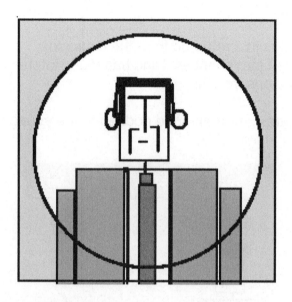

his lordship and his nephew both rose to greet mr
mahmoud. at a nod from his lordship, peters
departed.

"well, mr mahmoud," his lordship announced in his
most jovial manner, "something has come up that
could not wait until the official get together, eh?"

"there is something that i would like to discuss with
you privately, my lord," mr mahmoud replied evenly.

"permit mr to introduce my nephew - the duke of dent.
quite a healthy looking specimen of frankish young
manhood, isn't he? "

"indeed," mr mahmoud replied politely. "i am delighted to make your acquaintance, your grace. i am sure we can have a very pleasant conversation - after my private conversation with lord chandler is completed."

"david has just returned from the caucasus," continued lord chandler, "and has many interesting observations from his trip."

"i am sure." mr mahmoud nodded to the young duke.

"it is a great honor to meet you, sir," the duke addressed mr mahmoud smoothly. "i am sure i would like to plague you with a great many questions, more than courtesy might perhaps permit - " he smiled. "when the opportunity arises."

"i do not doubt, your grace, that you could tell me more than i could ever tell you."

and on that note the young duke left the room,
leaving the two elder statesmen to their parley.

lord chandler motioned to mr mahmoud to be seated.
"well, sir, may i offer you something? or shall we get
down to this unforeseen business."

mr mahmoud took the offered seat, seemingly more at
ease now that he had achieved his desired object of
getting lord chandler alone.

"i remember you had some excellent cherry brandy
when i last visited. that and some of your excellent
frankish coffee would be very welcome."

concealing his impatience, lord chandler rang for
peters.

22. the young duke

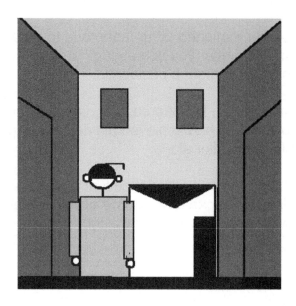

banished from the company of his uncle and mr
mahmoud, the duke of dent wandered through the
endless halls of the ancestral manse.

what a bore, he thought aimlessly. a few minutes ago
he had been dreading his uncle's tedious questions
about his, the duke's, trip to the caucasus. but now,
freed from that tiresomeness, he was wondering how
to best fill the hours before dinner.

a dinner he would have given anything to avoid. but,
what could you do?

how he wished bertha has agreed to come down for
the weekend! even with her gaggle of jackass
friends.

and if not bertha, at least beetle or cuthie or fat sally. someone he could at least talk to.

he heard voices in a room at the end of the corridor.

where was he? oh yes, one of the libraries. the one called "the library" although there were many others scattered through the old pile.

he recognized the voice of his young cousin angeline. who might she be talking to?

the governess, mademoiselle feval. yes, the duke thought, he might amuse himself twitting mademoiselle feval.

when he entered the room he saw, in addition to angeline and mademoiselle feval, two shabbily dressed strangers, a young woman and a younger man.

this did not surprise him. they might be journalists of some sort - although the man looked awfully young - or the pleaders of some dreary public cause, being humored by uncle william - or they might have simply wandered in. the old pile had always been liberty hall, in a manner that might shock the new breed of bureaucrats and politicians, with their mania for what they presumed to call "security".

"hullo, who have we here?," the duke announced himself. "who are these very special guests, angeline?"

"this is ms brown, and this handsome young fellow is mr smith."

the duke nodded to mary and joe. "it's a pleasure to meet you both," he smiled. "are you here on behalf of some worthy cause?" he sat down in an armchair in the corner, away from the window, beside a glass bookcase containing the 50 volumes of the memoirs of cardinal mandeville.

"they are here to fill out the dinner party," mademoiselle feval explained. "stone went out and found them on the roads."

"off course, of course, i should have guessed. well, i hope the dinner won't prove too tiresome an ordeal, and on behalf of lord chandler i thank you both."

"i am sure we will both enjoy it," mary replied. "the pleasure is ours."

the duke turned to angeline. "who are they replacing, by the way?"

"i am not sure," angeline frowned. "i was told, but i forgot."

"mr stafford and m sancerre, if i recall correctly.," said mademoiselle. "but don't hold me to it."

the duke nodded, and slouched deeper into his chair, suppressing a yawn.

"look here," said mademoiselle. "young mr smith here looks exactly the same size as you, your grace. why don't you see if you can find him something nice to wear for dinner? and i am about the same size as ms brown, i will do the same for her."

"well, if you think it necessary…" the duke drawled.

"well, i would not call it necessary, but we have had guests - so-called important guests - before, who have been a bit taken aback by his lordship's lack of ceremony."

angeline laughed. "and, david, look! mr smith is not just the same height and build as you, he looks just like you! you could be twins."

"do you really think so? " the duke replied uncertainly, looking over at joe. "not that i really know quite what i look like. not being the sort of chap who spends long hours in front of the looking glass."

23. peace and war

"this is really excellent," said mr mahmoud, and took another small sip of his coffee.

"i am glad you like it," lord chandler relied.

"well," mr mahmoud continued, finally surrenderng his cup to its saucer, " i will get to the point."

"please do."

"in a single word."

"which is?"

"war!"

"ah." lord chandler nodded. he had expected as much. what else could mr mahmoud have been about?

"i am sorry to have to announce it so suddenly." mr mahmoud put his fingertips together thoughtfully.

"i thought," lord chandler continued evenly, "that we had agreed on peace. as you had chosen to visit me, the leader of the peace party, rather than mr jefferson, the leader of the war party, i think the whole world had assumed the same."

"something has come up."

"no doubt. have you informed mr jefferson of your change of heart? or your change of plans, as the case may be."

"as you are in office, my lord, and not mr jefferson, i thought it proper to inform you first."

112

"yes. may i ask a favor of you?"

"you may ask," mr mahmoud replied.

"would you mind terribly postponing the announcement of hostilities for a day - or at least twelve hours - until i can inform mr jefferson? it would be the right thing to do. in out government we like to observe these little courtesies."

mr mahmoud shrugged. "the troops are already massing on the borders - "

"i ask you as a favor, mr mahmoud. a favor i am willing to repay personally. i repeat, that i am willing to repay *personally*."

"well, in that case, i am sure a delay - a delay of a day - can be arranged."

"thank you." lord chandler relaxed slightly and leaned back in his chair. "and now that has been settled, can you give me some details as to why this reversal has taken place?"

"an incident on the western border."

"i see. do you have any details as to this - incident?"

"some have been furnished me,"

"and do you feel at liberty to share them?"

"i do not see why not."

"good.' lord chandler sighed. "but before we proceed, i think i could use some brandy myself - and a cigar."

and lord chandler rang for peters once again.

24. a spot of bother

after it was decided that the duke would provide joe
with a suitable costume for dinner, and that angeline
would attempt to do the same for mary, the
conversation began to flag until mademoiselle feval
asked the duke,

"so what have you been up to, david? staying out of
mischief, i hope?"

the duke sighed. "i wish i could say i have. however,
i was mixed up in a spot of bother on my latest tour. "

"aren't you getting a little old for that sort of thing?"
mademoiselle asked. with a smile "i thought the
whole point of your being sent on these excursions
was to teach you to mind your manners among all
sorts and conditions of persons, and thus be able to
assume the responsibilities of your exalted position."

"yes, but it never seems to work out. trouble seems to follow me, like a shadow. and besides, i do not see that i have such an exalted position, as you put it, as all that."

"your uncle seems to think so, and his is the opinion that counts, at least for now," mademoiselle replied.

"but tell us, david," angeline said. "what exactly was this 'spot of bother'? do not keep us in suspense. unless it was too sordid to recount in civilized company. or heaven forbid, that it involved so-called 'state security'."

"oh, i would not go so far as to claim that," said the duke, with a slightly uneasy laugh. "but, look here, let me tell you the tale, and you can decide as to its sordidness."

"please do," angeline encouraged him, with a glance at the other listeners.

"well, i was staying in a little town in the middle of nowhere, on the border of somewhere or other. i had been traveling by train, the way uncle wishes me to, as you know. i had met a fellow on the train in somewhat the same situation as my own, and he seemed a pleasant enough chap, though not overly bright. but i don't care much for bright people and we got along all right. like i say, a pleasant enough chap, though he did not seem to hold his liquor very well."

"but as i assume you were not consuming as much liquor as all that," angeline interjected, "i do not suppose that presented much of a problem."

"no, of course not."

"did this amiable personage have a name?" angeline asked.
"gregor, his name was gregor. he was the heir to some sort of manufacturing fortune."

117

"yes, people named gregor usually are,"

"anyway, gregor and i decided to stay for the night in this little town , in its little old-fashioned hostelry. and, wouldn't you know it, there was some sort of festival going on, with all the townsfolk in some sort of strange costumes."

"actually, i would not know it," said angeline. "but please go on."

"a festival?" asked mademoiselle feval, "it must have been a very out of the way place. i would have thought such things were completely obsolete."

"oh, i think they only had it once a year," said the duke. "i am sure they spent the rest of the year indoors watching television like the rest of the human race."

"and you and your new friend just happened to come along on the one day of the year," said angeline.

"indeed we did. do you want me to go on?"

"of course. i am sorry to keep interrupting. it is a bad habit of mine, one of many that poor mademoiselle has been hired to cure me of."

"anyway," the duke continued," gregor and i went out into the town square just as the sun was going down, and it seemed that a young man and a young woman of the town had just been elected, or acclaimed, as the king and queen of the festival, and they were standing above the crowd on some kind of platform. "

the duke paused , as if expecting some comment from angeline, but she only raised her eyebrows slightly, so he went on.

25. yara

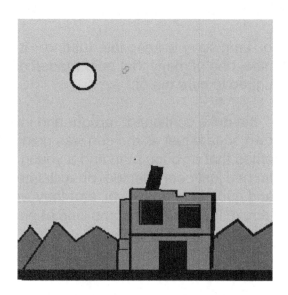

the village of r————— had for many centuries
been the most damned and desolate place on earth.

there was a little inn outside the village, on the long
road leading to the imperial capital.

every year moloch, old nick, the wandering jew,
sinbad the sailor, the whore of babylon, the prankster,
and the fool met at the inn.

nobody knew exactly why, but they did.

old zashaw, the innkeeper, was always very attentive
to his curiously assorted guests.

as good as their custom was - and they spent far more freely than his usual guests, especially sinbad and the whore of babylon - he was always relieved when they packed up and departed and he could relax for another dreary year.

zashaw had trouble retaining help, but one year he happened to have staying with him, his young great grand-daughter.

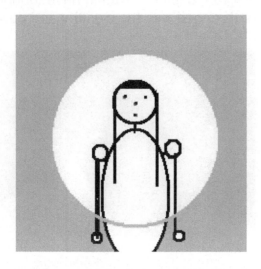

her name was yara. she was a beautiful raven haired child of about seven years of age, and her notable comeliness attracted the notice of the guests, particularly the whore of babylon and the prankster, as they sat around the big table of the inn, waiting to be served their first meal after their arrival.

"this child," opined the whore to old zashaw, "is too beautiful to spend her life in this backwater. surely some passing prince will purchase her, either for himself or some faithful and favoured courtier."

zashaw smiled. after years of waiting on his somewhat frightful guests, he was never sure of when they were serious or when they were chaffing him. "you may think so, madam, but in fact no princes or courtiers ever travel this way, so your prediction is not that likely to come to pass."

"you do not say so," interposed the prankster. "so close to the great capital? i would have thought the roads were thronged with the wealthy and powerful?"

"the road from the south, perhaps, leading to the capital," the old innkeeper murmured, "but on this side of the city the road leads only north to ice and desolation." what he did not add was, he had always assumed that the seven chose his inn because it was out of the way.

"be that as it may," said the whore, "i predict that this child will be carried off by a handsome prince, who will make her his princess. what say you all?" she asked the other guests.

"a prince?" cried the fool in his his high voice. "a king, no less! this maiden shall live to be a queen and rule a mighty kingdom!"

the other guests nodded, already bored with the conversation, and old zashaw, assisted by the child, continued to take their orders and serve them, and there the matter seemed to be forgotten.

except by the cook, one of zashaw's grandaughters, who had big ears and had been listening from the kitchen.

little yara was her stepdaughter, and the cook, jealous of the child's unearthly beauty, took every opportunity to box her ears or thrash her if she, the cook, thought the child was putting on airs or was developing ideas above her station.

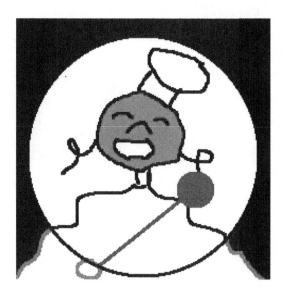

"a queen, eh?" the cook greeted yara when she returned to the kitchen, "i fear that idea will have to be beaten out of you, my sweet child. what say you, grandfather?" she asked zashaw when he arrived behind the child.

"i say mind your pots, you fat baggage," the old man replied. "and make sure the soup is nice and hot, and the roasts well turned, the way our guests like it. let us keep them happy, and all else will take care of itself.

yara smiled to herself at this exchange - though there was no guarantee the cook would not smack her sooner or later - and exchanged a quick glance with her only friend - zeus, the black tomcat who was co-ruler of the kitchen.

the meal was served and life at the inn went on without further incident.

except that yara grew more beautiful with every passing month, and year.

26. the prince

true to her word, carla the cook gave yara a sound
thrashing the next day, after the seven guests had
left.

yara did not care. she knew that some day, probably
some day soon, either the handsome young prince
would come and take her away, or the sky would open
up and a golden bird or dragon would carry her away
to her own kingdom.

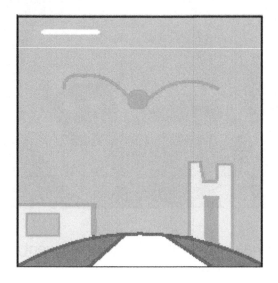

it was only a matter of time. of waiting.

and carla the cook would get hers. that is, if yara
could even be bothered with her.

meanwhile, life went on at the inn, with yara
performing such duties as were required of her by old
zashaw and by carla. but as business was slow,
these duties were not too onerous, and yara spent

much of her time dreaming of the beautiful future which surely awaited her.

the only question was, which would come first, the golden bird or dragon, or the prince?

or perhaps none of them would come, and when yara was old enough in a few years time she would simply take to the highway herself and conquer her own kingdom - the one which her beauty entitled her to.

on one particularly cold, dreary, and rainy evening, the prince arrived.

he arrived with only a few attendants, and in a plain carriage and wearing plain clothing as if he were attempting to be incognito, but he fooled nobody.

not old zashaw, not carla or murgle the maid or samson the stable boy, and especially not yara, who knew right away that her prince, and her time, had come.

the prince's attendants - two stout dark visaged fellows who looked as if they had fought in many a battle - carried his bags up to the best room in the inn under the guidance of murgle, while zashaw, with the assistance of samson, prepared as cheerful and blazing a fire as he could in the dining room.

the crafty zashaw kept yara out of sight for the moment, waiting until the prince was as comfortable as he could be made, before blinding him with the sight of the maid.

the prince looked on disinterestedly as the the fire was stoked.

"please, your highness, make yourself comfortable," zashaw smiled ingratiatingly and pulled a chair away from the table. "ours is a poor establishment, but i hope you will find our fare hearty at least."

"what is this 'hignness'? i am no prince, nor king nor duke either. were you expecting some prince? you must have confused me with him," the prince replied easily as he seated himself. "very flattering, to be sure.

"no - sir, we were expecting no one in particular," zashaw quiclkly rejoindered. "it is just that your - your bearing, sir - led me to think you a gentleman of some consequence."

"indeed." the prince stripped his gloves of and placed them on the table., revealing long powerful swordsman's hands a bit at odds with his otherwise somewhat delicate appearance. "in any case, hearty fare, if you can provide it, is the best fare, as we have a long journey ahead of us."

"to be sure, sir.   and your men, too, shall have hearty fare in the kitchen."

"they are not my men, they are my comrades. they will dine with me."

"of course, sir, as you wish. i will have places prepared for them."

yara heard and watched all this from a crack in the door to the kitchen . behind her she could feel the heat of the stove, and of the basilisk stare of clara.

27. the mission

yara watched the prince as he stared down at the table, drumming his long swordsman's fingers on it.

she wished she could read his thoughts. not that she did not have confidence in her ability to bewitch any man.

behind her she could hear the geese roasting on the spit under the watchful eye of clara, who was also watching yara.

the prince's thoughts - for despite his disclaimers, he was indeed a prince - were gloomy ones.

he was on a mission from his father, the king of d — — — —, to offer terms of surrender to the emperor of a— — — — —, who demanded that the kingdom of d — — — — — recognize him as their liege lord, and pay him a yearly ransom of gold, horses, maidens, and precious stones.

the kingdom of d————, though small and hidden in remote hills, had long prided itself on its fierce independence. but with the increasing power of the empire of a..........., the elderly monarch thought it prudent to not defy its might, but to bide his time until the empire might be weakened by its rivalries with the equally aggressive empires on its eastern and southern borders.

needless to say this did not sit well with the hot blooded young prince and his coterie of hot blooded young followers, who lusted for the glory of war.

the prince had spoken half the truth to zashaw when he described his two companions as his "comrades".

one of them, arbo, was his old master at arms, an old and loyal follower of the king who had taught the prince the arts of war and swordsmanship. a more loyal and stout fellow could not be found.

the other, terno, had been assigned to the prince by the king's crafty vizier and favorite, duke warko, as a spy, to make sure the prince executed his disagreeable commission.

arbo and terno were to play the role of humble servants in the prince's incognito, but the prince had little patience with the details of the masquerade, as evidenced by his assertion to zashaw that they should share his table.

when arbo and terno came down to the dining room and took their places at the table, zashaw, at a signal from yara, brought out two bottles of his "best" wine, such as was, and glasses.

zashaw assured the trio that the roast geese - his "famous" roast geese, famous throughout this humble corner of the world- would be served shortly, and begged their patience. his effusive obsequiousness was met with absent nods.

the innkeeper retired to the kitchen after attending to the fire, and the prince and his two companions sipped their wine in silence.

then yara entered with the platter of geese.

28. the conquest

then yara entered with the platter of geese.

the prince glanced at her - and then stood up.

"my princess!" he gasped. "my queen!"

yara favored the prince with the briefest of smiles as
she approached the table, as if to indicate that such
compliments were an every day occurrence for her, or
perhaps that she had not even understood the
prince's words, and was only smiling as she would to
any guest.

the faithful arbo had seen such displays on the
prince's part before, though perhaps never one
occasioned by one so young as yara.

"sit down, sir," he admonished the prince gently. "we have a part to play," he added in a whisper.

yara placed the platter on the table. the prince, however, did not sit down but continued to stare at her

.

""innkeeper!" arbo cried. hoping to break the spell, "fill our glasses if you please."

zashaw had been watching from behind the kitchen door, and he responded as quickly as he could.

"but, sir," he said to arbo when he had brought the wine out, "i see your glasses are all filled. i filled them but a few minutes ago."

arbo drained his glass and slammed it in the table in front of him.

"enough of this nonsense!" cried the prince, finally taking his eyes from yara. "it is no wine we want but this maid. tell me, sir innkeeper, what is your price for her?"

"the maid?" zashaw glanced at yara casually, as if noticing her existence for the first time. "why, sir, as to that," he replied smoothly, though taken a bit aback by catching his prey so quickly and so completely, "i would not say that, strictly speaking, she is for sale.. she is but a child after all, my own flesh and blood, and a sacred trust - "

"how much do you want for her?" the prince interrupted him. "no nonsense, sir, none of your palavering with me! i am prince a——————, heir to the kingdom of d——————, and i will have this creature for my queen at any price."

at this arbo and terno threw up their hands in despair. "come, innkeeper." terno managed to say, "you can see that the young man is not to be denied. give us a fair price, and let us be done with this business, so that we may enjoy our dinner."

clara the cook and murgle the stable boy had been watching and listening from behind the kitchen door, and at the prince's passionate admission clara turned to murgle wth a grin of triumph.

"i have her now!" she exclaimed, "wait you here, murgle, and mind the kitchen. i have business to attend to."

for clara, like many other servants in establishments great and small along the highway to the capital of the empire, was paid a few pennies a month to be a spy for the imperial police.

throwing a shawl around her shoulders,she hastened out the back door of the in in search of the local bailiff, sure that her information would prove interesting to him.

at the very least yara's chances of being carried off by the prince would be foiled. perhaps she could be implicated in a plot against the emperor - and hanged as a spy or burned as a witch!

29. on the run

ernestine got up from the sofa. as she did, the doorbell rang.

whoever can that be, she wondered.

she walked slowly over to the door and looked through the peephole.

she saw a little man wearing an overcoat two sizes too large for him, sort of weaselly looking but not very threatening.

how did this creature get in here, she wondered, i will have to berate the management. or maybe not, what a bore.

she opened the door suddenly. "i believe you have the wrong door," she told the little weaselly man. "you have no business with anybody here."

"is jemmy here?" the little man asked, in no way abashed by ernestine's forceful declaration.

"jemmy is most assuredly not here," ernestine replied with a smile.

"jemmy, are you in there?" the little man called.

jeremy appeared behind ernestne. "what is it, raffy?" he asked. "it must be serious, for you to come here. i hope it is."

"oh, it is serious, jem. hobie has spilled the beans to gumm, and it's all up. gumm is probably right behind me, so we have to make tracks fast."

"good heavens, what is all this?" exclaimed ernestine. "jeremy, do you mean to tell me you know this person?"

"yes, i am afraid i do, my dear."

"but - i don't understood. you are a respected member of the opposition party. and this little fellow is - "

"come, my dear," jeremy laughed. "don't play the innocent. i have a secret life, like most human beings, as i am sure you do yourself. i just happen to have got caught, that's all. now if you will excuse me ."

jeremy turned back to the title man he had addressed as "raffy". "i assume you have a car outside."

but another voice interrupted him "not so fast, jem."

a man appeared behind raffy, a hulking bearlike brute with a small head, a wide hat, and a scowl on his round features.

"oh there you are, bootsie," jeremy drawled. "hold on, i will be right with you, as soon as i get my coat."

"never mind that gammon, jem. what about her?" he gestured with his thumb at ernestine.

"oh, you don't have to worry about ernie, she won't peach. will you, my dear?"

"i am not sure what i would 'peach' about" ernestine answered.

"she will have to come with us," bootsie announced.

jeremy shrugged. "she night be in the way."

"i will be the judge of that," bootsie answered.

"well," jeremy laughed pleasantly, "it looks like we have a standoff."

"majority rules," bootsie countered.   we will let raffy decide. what say you, raffy? shall we take her or leave her?"

raffy took his time answering, looking ernestine up and down. "she's a right foxy-looking bird, though a bit long on the tooth. i say we take her."

jeremy sighed. "let us get our coats, my dear," he told ernestine.

"but -"

"come, come, it has been decided. you might enjoy it. you have always said you wished for more excitement in your life."

30. king and queen

a young man and a young woman of the town had just been elected, or acclaimed, as the king and queen of the festival, and they were standing above the crowd on some kind of platform.

gregor and the young duke of dent, who had advised gregor to address him familiarly as david, wandered through the milling crowd toward the platform.

though most of the crowd were in their colorful native costumes, no one seemed to take any particular notice of gregor and david in their plain hiking gear.

gregor noticed a young woman in the crowd, apparently alone, who was dressed in casual traveling clothes, not in costume. he steered his way toward her with david in tow.

"hullo there," gregor addressed the young woman in the familiar way he had with everyone, "i say, do you know what this is all about?"

seen up close, the woman was not quite as young as gregor and david had first thought. they noticed that she had a little notebook in one hand and a pencil in the other. she looked at gregor as if barely registering his existence.

"it is a ceremony, " she said, "an annual ceremony on the anniversary of great event in the history of the town."

"and what might that great event have been?" gregor asked with a smile.

"a prince carried away a village maid and this started a great war which resulted in the village being free from tyranny forever," the woman told gregor. " the prince became a king and the maid became his queen."

"that sounds jolly," gregor agreed.

"not quite so jolly as all that. for you see, the story did
not end there. for when the war was over and the
people had been freed, both the king snd queen grew
bored and distracted after the tumultuous events
which had transformed the world of its time. the king
spent more and more time with his mighty men,
hunting stags in the deep wood , and banging
tankards on the tables in every high and low inn in the
kingdom. the queen for her part became quite
friendly with a young page at the court, a nephew of
one of the kings dethroned in the great war. well, you
can guess what happened next."

"the king caught the queen and the page boy and
killed one or both of them to redeem his honor,"

gregor replied, "because those were the good old days."

"close, but not exactly. the king did indeed run his good sword through the bodies of both lovers, but when he did the queen turned into a red bird and flew away to the east and the page turned into a green bird and flew away to the west . legend has it that one day the two birds will return and when they do a volcano will erupt beneath the kingdom and destroy it."

"oh dear," laughed gregor ,"that does not sound promising at all."

"so what is the point of the ceremony?" the young duke asked the woman with the notebook.

"every year the murder of the queen by the king is reenacted, and supposedly this keeps the birds from returning for another year."

"you do not mean to say," cried the duke, "that a young woman is actually killed in this ceremony! how dreadful!"

gregor and the woman both laughed at the young man's outburst. "no, of course not," the woman assured him. "it is only a little play, a charade, that lasts hardly ten minutes,

the duke blushed. "no, of course not, what was i thinking? but, tell me, how seriously do you think these villagers take all this."

"how seriously does anyone take anything these days? after all, these villagers are just inhabitants of the modern world like everyone else, hearing the same news and watching the same shows as everyone else. once a year they dress up for this, for the rest of the year they probably never hear or speak a harsh word but just go about their business."

"yes," sighed gregor. "this modern world can not be accused of skimping on dreariness. but look here, are you some kind of journalist? i could not help noticing the little notebook you are flourishing."

"i am indeed," the woman replied. "i am carlotta bligh, of the international news service, at your service."

"carlotta bligh!" exclaimed gregor. "why of course! we should have recognized you, shouldn't we have, old boy? what a great honor!"

"you probably thought i was dead," carlotta replied with a smile. "my fame, like that of most of my colleagues on the international beat, is not what it was."

"nonsense! you are as famous as ever," gregor cried gallantly. "the fault is all ours, for not recognizing you."

gregor and the duke proceeded to properly introduce themselves, as the trio continued to approach the stage in the middle of the square.

31. damages

"so there you have it," mr mahmoud finished his tale. "in addition to the damage caused, the two young rascals seriously impugned the honor of the ancient kingdom of s............., which, obscure aa it may be, is nonetheless a member, indeed a founding member of the alliance i have the honor to be the spokesperson for."

lord chandler sighed. "and these damages that you refer to, what exactly do they amount to, in pounds and drachmas?"

mr mahmoud waved his hand . "they are nothing. they are of no account. it is the honor of one of the members of our alliance that is of concern."

"of course. still, if you could be so kind as to write the amount of the damages on a slip of paper, i will write a cheque for it, payable by my government and made out to bearer. i trust you can put it in the right hands."

"i would be honored."

"that part is settled, then. now, what else does the kingdom of s………. desire, to satisfy its honor?'

"it wants the two miscreants returned to face public trial."

"i see. well, i may be a bit prejudiced, but i know that my nephew, the young duke of d——, is what you might call a languid young man, not at all demonstrative or given to violent expressions - of - much of anything. as a duke, hardly less than asa member of loyalty, he has been trained in the art of graciousness. i venture to say it was much more likely that the other young chap involved - and i am not sure exactly who or what he was - was the true culprit. of course, a full investigation should be made." lord chandler cleared his throat. "perhaps a special commission, that sort of thing."

mr mahmoud laughed gently. "i think the time or special commissions has passed, my lord. also, if i may say so, think putting the blame on the other young man will not be much to the purpose."

"and why not?" lord chandler replied with a bare hint of annoyance. "who is he, anyway? and what nation is he from?"

"that is the problem. he belongs to no nation. he is the nephew and heir of mr n——————, the chief stockholder of the nautilus conglomerate. not exactly untouchable, but close enough. and of course the nautilus conglomerate is hardly known to the peasantry and inspires neither awe nor loathing."

"oh, dear," agreed lord chandler. "i see what you mean."

"and there is another factor," mr mahmoud continued, with a gleam in his eye. "the oldest factor of all."

"oh?"

"a woman!"

"a woman? my nephew did not mention a young woman."

"not a young woman. but a woman you may have heard of , or remember - none other than carlotta bligh."

"carlotta bligh!" lord chandler exclaimed. "i thought the world had been well rid of carlotta bligh years ago."

"apparently not. she is probably preparing her version of events even as we speak. at the very least, she will surely make it impossible to make the whole incident disappear."

lord chandler sighed. "i think i need to talk to my nephew again. when i have finished with him, we can resume this conversation. is that agreeable to you?"

mr mahmoud smiled. "of course."

"perhaps we can meet again over breakfast."

"i would prefer, my lord, to come to an understanding tonight."

"very well. as you wish."

32. an unfamiliar theme

"well, i must admit your new friend behaved quite
foolishly, but i do not see why any great fuss should
be made about it, " angeline observed after the duke
finished his tale. " international incident indeed! or
why you should be held accountable, as you seem to
have done what you could to stop him."

"at least by your own account," mademoiselle feval
added dryly.

joe and mary had listened politely to the duke's story,
without commenting or interrupting. joe had had
trouble making any sense of it, but mary observed,

"and what of ms carlotta bligh? is she being blamed or implicated in this episode? as according to your account, she was accompanying you? i must admit i am particularly curious, as i have always been an ardent admirer of that intrepid personage."

"miss bligh disappeared after the incident," the duke replied. "neither gregor nor myself, when detained and questioned by the authorities, fell it incumbent on us to mention her presence."

"that was gallant of you," angeline observed, but before she could expand or the theme, or the duke reply, the little party was interrupted by the arrival of peters, lord chandler's manservant..

"lord chandler requests your presence, your grace," peters addressed the duke. "he asked me to tell you it was most urgent."

with a sigh, the duke rose, made his apologies, and followed peters out of the room.

to joe's and mary's eyes, neither angeline nor mademoiselle feval seemed to place any great import on the urgency of lord chandler's summons.

"tell me, ms brown," angeline asked, "who is this carlotta bligh person whom you describe yourself as an ardent admirer of? the name seems to ring a distant bell."

"she was - and apparently still is - a foreign correspondent, traveling over the globes and galaxies in hopes of getting the real stories behind developing stories."

"i see." angeline replied in a tone that plainly said that stated that she did not see at all. "but what exactly is a story if it is not itself? and in any case any story is available to anyone who cares to take the time to interest themselves in it."

"and," added mademoiselle feval, "in any case there are millions of new stories every day, washing away the ones of the previous day. so who needs some so-called foreign correspondent to tell them what to look at? of course," she added in a gentler tone to mary, "if ms bligh was some sort of childhood hero to you, that is another matter, and quite understandable."

"although, " angeline addressed mary, "i must say you seem a bit young to remember the heyday of such an old trouper as carlotta bligh."

"my mother was an enthusiastic admirer of carlotta bligh," mary replied. "not only in her capacity as a foreign correspondent, but as one of the last of the great feminists."

" a feminist!" exclaimed mademoiselle feval. "why it is ages since i heard the term."

"but what is a feminist?" asked angeline. "is it some some of person? i thought is was some sort of jewel, or maybe a flower or a fruit."

"oh no," mademoiselle feval laughed. "they were people all right. very - very - very forceful people, many of them. very much inclined to put themselves forward."

"and still are," mary added, perhaps a shade too loudly for polite conversation, "i, myself, am a feminist!"

"you do not say so!" exclaimed mademoiselle feval. "how droll! why, this is wonderful! when you mentioned starting a new religion i must admit i rolled my third eye a bit, but a feminist! well, this will provide a wonderful topic of conversation at dinner, if you do not mind expounding on the theme to mr mahmoud and our other guests, who often find themselves at a loss for a fresh or unfamiliar theme."

"i do not mind in the least , " mary answered. "i should be happy to expound, as you put it, on the subject, if that is your desire."

"then it is settled. how fortunate we were to find you, ms brown. i now look forward to dinner, which i must confess i had been mildly dreading."

"mary smiled. "it will be my pleasure."

joe had no idea what they were talking about, and kept his own counsel, as usual.

33. the double

lord chandler realized there was no use remonstrating with the young duke, however much he felt exasperated with him. he maintained his usual urbane tone, as he descried the conversation he had had with mr mahmoud.

"it seems, david," his lordship casually intoned, "that some concession must be made to the sensibilities of the offended kingdom. and the easiest concession, and the one most distinctly seen as a concession, is that you should return to the kingdom to face trial for the terrible offense of defiling their time honored custom."

the duke blinked perplexedly. "but - explain to me, again, uncle, what is to be gained? according to you, war is to be declared in any case! it is only a matter of days."

"that is true, david. your grasp of the situation is admirable, and bodes well for your future in diplomacy. but, you must also be aware that in situations like this, when armies must be massed on borders and fleets sent forth on the seas, days, even hours are crucial." his lordship smiled. "after all, it is not as if you are likely to actually be shot, or hanged, even if you are found guilty. after the formalities have been observed, and war declared, the usual channels, aboveground and not so aboveground, will open up, and with some judicious negotiations, whose lubrication i am willing to *personally* guarantee, you should return safe and sound, with some excellent material for your memoirs."

"but - hang it all, uncle, it is easy for you to say that it is not *likely* that i shall be shot or hanged - but, oh dear, what a bother! what a bore1"

lord chandler shrugged. "it is the chance we shall
have to take. fortune of war, and so forth. unless you
have some other idea?"

"but - yes. yes, i do. an idea, by george, that just
popped into my head."

with the faintest of smiles, lord chandler replied, "and
what might that be?"

"well, you know how in novels and plays chaps who
are doubles of some other chap are always playing
the part of the first chap so that he can be in two
places in once, or go in a secret mission or
something?"

"actually i do not quite know, but go on."

"suppose i found a fellow who looked just like me -
could we not send him to the kingdom of s — — — — —

in my place? if he agreed to do it for a reasonable price, or - or just for the spirit of the thing? would that not be capital?"

lord chandler could not help laughing. "and are you prepared to put your hand on such a fellow - on such short notice?"

"as a matter of fact, i can. he fell from the heavens just a few hours ago, when wallace went out looking for someone to make up tonight's party. the fellow could be my twin. it must be fate. you will see him at dinner, and i am sure you will agree."

"very well, david, i will take a look at this heaven-sent personage." his lordship smiled tolerantly. "but i think it might still be best if you prepared yourself mentally for a return to the kingdom of s — — — — —.

34. dinner for twelve

"you miserable gutless wretch," mrs stafford hissed at mr stafford. "this is positively the last indignity i suffer at your weak hands. when we leave here we go our separate ways, and this time i mean it."

"darling, the problem is not that i don't have guts, but that i do, " mr stafford replied, lying on the sofa of their suite, with a towel over his eyes. "surely you don't want me to do something on mrs foster's clean white tablecloth, that she probably pays more to launder than we can hope to scratch up I'm a year."

"yes, and we will go on scratching year after year, if you can't play up and play the game just when the fighting is hottest. after all the work and scheming i put into getting this invitation - i don't know what to say. except that you disgust me."

"i can disgust you, darling," mr staffed replied. "but nobody else seems to be paying the least bit of attention to us, no matter how much work you put into getting the invitation."

"no, because you won"t make any effort to get their attention. how are lord chandler and the other guests to notice you if you stay in bed with a rag over your face?"

mr stafford sighed, but did not respond further.

"i am going downstairs now," mrs stafford announced. "i give you one last chance to play the man."

"enjoy your dinner."

"very well, then." mrs stafford left the room.

she stood outside the door for about half a minute,
but there were no sounds from within from mr stafford.

nor did anyone else appear in the corridor. she
headed for the wide staircase, and as she did so, the
frown vanished from her face and was replaced by a
satisfied smile.

*

mr stafford waited for two minutes after mrs stafford
closed the door behind her, then got up, and opened
the door to make sure she was not lurking outside.

he saw. on the other side of the great staircase,
another of the guests - what was her name, daisy
something? - approaching the head of the stairs, but
barely glanced at her and went back into the room
and closed the door behind him.

the dinner proceeded with the smoothness only
possible when neither the host nor any of the guests
cared whether it did or not.

to mrs foster it was just another dinner to host for her
long time friend lord chandler.

lord chandler and mr mahmoud had weighty affairs of
state - if not the fate of civilization - on their plate, and
were happy to be free of them for a couple of hours,
no matter how bland or boring the conversation.

m chan, mr mahmoud's assistant, also had affairs of
state on his mind, albeit at one remove, but was in
fact quite hungry and looking forward to feeding
himself.

the duke of dent also had something on his mind -
the damned awkward business of his trip to the
kingdom of s.............. what a bother!

mrs stafford was in a good mood, feeling she was
had achieved her purpose in getting invited to the
dinner - getting well rid of mr stafford, and much more
easily than she had hoped.

joe and mary did not know what to expect, and were
more than happy just to be getting fed.

to angeline and mlle feta, it was just another night.

and the two remaining guests, the ubiquitous mrs
cream and the slightly mysterious darcy filbertson,
were just happy to be there.

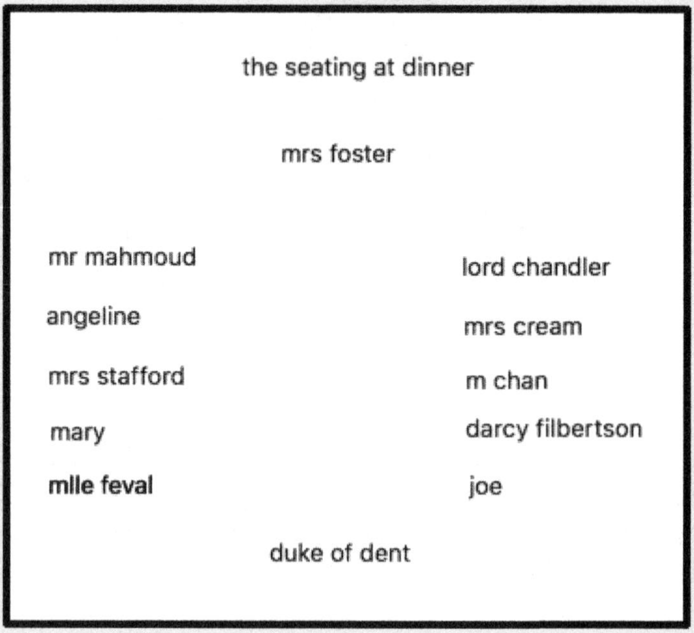

the seating at dinner

mrs foster

mr mahmoud

lord chandler

angeline

mrs cream

mrs stafford

m chan

mary

darcy filbertson

mlle feval

joe

duke of dent

35. "i say we go ahead"

the motor was running in the car outside in the street in front of ernestine's apartment.

there was no sign of the doorman, ernestine noted.

the big man, bootsie, got in beside the driver.

the little man, raffy, got in the back seat and moved over behind the driver. jeremy indicated to ernestine that she should get in next, and then he followed her and closed the door and the car sped off immediately, powerfully and smoothly.

the back seat was quite wide, and at least ernestine was not crushed between raffy and jeremy.

the car sailed through the dark streets. nobody spoke until they were out of the city limits.

"well, this exciting," jeremy spoke art last. "i assume we are still going through with it, just a little ahead of schedule."

"going through with it!" boots exclaimed. "are you stark raving mad? no - you're joking, of course. this is no time for your jokes, jem."

"but i am serious, boots. what have we to lose, eh? old bill will never expect us to pull to ff now. instead of moving fast, they are probably taking their time and getting up enough troops to invade a planet. i say i phone staff, tell it's a go, but be on the alert, we might be there earlier than expected."

"what say, you, raft?" boots looked over his shoulder and asked the little man.

"don't ask me, boots, i/m just a foot soldier. whatever you gents decide, that's right with me."

"and you, daff?" boots asked the driver.

daff? thought ernestine. short for daffy? what a crew!

the driver answered in a woman's voice, an almost cultured voice. "i like jem's idea. i say we go for it. i will have to put the pedal to the metal though , we can't be worried about speed limits and such."

"right ho!" jeremy replied to the driver's speech. "you always were a trump, daphne."

"all right then, jem," said boots. "i tell you what - we wild it your way. but if it goes wrong, before bill gets the chance to put the metal on us, i will strangle you with my own hands. how does that suit you?"

"well enough," jeremy answered. "i could not ask fairer than that. now let me call staffy." he took his phone out of his pocket.

*

so far , so good, thought mr stafford, as he closed the door behind them.

he went over and sat on the little settee in the room and took outhit his phone to check the time.

jem or raffy should be calling any minute.

the phone   rang in his hand.

right on schedule. everything must be going right, he thought

36. lost

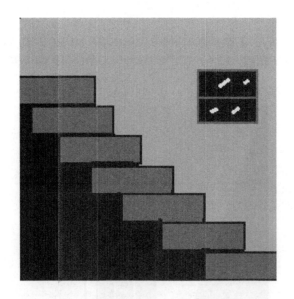

"are you lost, sir? these are the working areas of the
staff, and those stairs you seem about to descend
are the back stairs."   rogers, the under -butler,
smiled pleasantly at mr stafford.

mr stafford smiled back at rogers, just as pleasantly.

"no, i just wanted a little privacy."

"very good, sir. and you did not find the room
provided you had privacy enough?"

"not for the purpose i required, no."

rogers nodded. "i see, sir."

"do you not want to know what my purpose is."

"you can tell me if you like, sir."

"i wanted to count my money."

"ah! always a worthwhile endeavor, sir and as you infer, one best done in the most complete privacy."

mr stafford reached into his pocket. "would you like to see how much money i have?"

"that is up to you, sir."

"i always carry money - cash - in case i have a sudden desire to contribute to charity."

"i believe charity is recommended by all faiths and philosophies , sir."

"yes. all those that count, anyway. tell me, rogers - i believe that is your name is it not - "

"it is, sir.

"do you have a favorite charity?"

rogers hesitated before replying. "i have some, sir,
but if i may be so bold as to say so, i suspect that
something more is involved here than one person or
another's favorite charity."

"ha, ha! i see you are a sharp fellow, rogers, wth no
moss growing between your ears. what, then do you
think i might be up to?   do you think i might wish to
rob mrs foster?"

"i do not know what you could find it worth your while
to rob her of, sir. surely you realize she does not
keep any appreciable amount of cash or jewelry in the
house. her wine cellar is acceptable at best. nor does
she have any so-called priceless works of art on
hand. in ant case, my limited understanding is that
such things are not at all what they used to be."

"very good, rogers, very good. tell me, how would you like to be part of making history ?"

rogers raised his eyebrows ever so slightly. "history, sir?

"well, the nightly news, at least. as you surely know, two of mrs foster's guests tonight are lord chandler and m. mahmoud. "

"i am as aware f that as you are, sir."

"i will let you in on a little secret. i am a member of a so-called 'mob' which is going to kidnap lord chandler and m mahmoud tonight and perhaps change the course of history. my confederates are speeding towards us even as we speak. what do you think of that, eh"

"i must confess such a proceeding might get people's attention."

"how would you like to bring a little excitement into our life and go in with us? become part of our gang?"

"begging your pardon, sir, are you not being a bit presumptuous in assuming my life lacks excitement?"

"oh, i meant no offense, i assure you." just then mr stafford's phone rang and he hastily took it out of his pocket. "excuse me."

37. a brief history

mrs stafford could hardly wait for the dinner, and the evening, to be over, so that she could start packing, and be ready to slip out of mrs foster's house at the crack of dawn.

on her way to a proper celebration of her freedom - at last! - from mr stafford and all his useless schemes.

meanwhile there was the dinner to be gotten through. she did not care how bland the food might be. or how boring the guests at table.

she found herself three seats from the hostess's right, between mrs foster's daughter angeline, and a young woman she did not know, and who did not look quite comfortable in her clothes, as if they had been provided for her for the dinner.

mrs stafford smiled at the unknown young woman. "i do not believe we've met."

"i am sure we have not," mary replied.

"this is ms brown, mrs stafford," mademoiselle feval, the governess, seated on mary's right, said. "i am relying on her to make the conversation at dinner interesting."

"oh?" mrs stafford replied politely. "and why might that be?"

"you will never guess what ms brown is," mademoiselle feval continued.

"i am sure that i can not," mrs stafford smiled.

"she is a feminist! and - she aspires to start her own religion."

"well, one meets persons starting new religions everywhere - but a feminist! that is interesting, " mrs stafford agreed. "though I am afraid i have forgotten quite what a feminist is - though i am sure i must have learned it at school."

"that is what many people think, and say," mary smiled back at mrs stafford. "and i think the reason for that is that they are taught that feminism triumphed in the previous centuries and that therefore there is no more need of it. nothing, however, could be further from the truth."

"you do not say so," mademoiselle feval prompted mary.

"i do say so," mary replied. "the other thing people do not realize is that feminism, so far from being something completely unheard of that suddenly emerged from nowhere in the preceding centuries, has its origins in what is commonly misunderstood as quote prehistory unquote, and is in fact iitself the true prehistory of the human race, or what is left of it, after the ravages of millenia of patriarchy. "

"that sounds like a most interesting theory," mrs stafford. "you must have done a great deal of research to support it."

"i have indeed. but perhaps the best place to commence my account is not with my own researches, but with the story of matriarchy itself - how it came to be, and how it came to be buried for thousands of years."

"do go on, please," mademoiselle feval urged.

*

mademoiselle feval, mrs stafford, and darcy filbertson, seated directly across from mary, listened attentively to mary's recital.

angeline, seated on mrs stafford's left, also listented to mary with one ear while also listening politely and making an occasional interjection to the small talk betwee mr mahmoud, on her left, and mrs foster, who sat at the head of the table.

lord chandler ignored mrs cream, who in her turn kept up a steady stream of cutural commentary to m chan, who nodded at proper intervals while enjoying his dinner.

the young duke, at the foot of the table, conversed with joe, seated directly on his right, in his , the duke's, friendliest manner.

"what do you think of the old pile, eh?" the duke asked joe. "must seen pretty dreary to a young chap like yourself, used to a life of adventure."

joe did not know how to reply,

"it's big," he finally said

38. the gamblers

charles's "little more private place" was a small 24
hour coffee shop a couple of blocks away from the
berkeley bank.

There were no customers in the place, and nobody
behind the counter, when charles and magnus and
johnny entered.

after charles called out, a little old man came out from
the back and they each bought a cup of coffee.   then
the little man disappeared, leaving them alone in a
booth near the door.

charles proceeded to give magnus and johnny a very
brief account of his history with the berkeley bank,
and then made his proposition to them.

"so there you have it," charles concluded. "what do you think?'

"uh - it's a lot to take in," magnus told him.

"i understand that," said charles. "but consider the possible payoff. come, gentlemen, you are both gamblers, are you not?"

"i gamble sometimes," magnus agreed. "but i consider myself basically a sage."

"of course, of course," charles quickly reassured him. "i didn't mean anything negative by calling you a gambler - just the opposite, ha ha!"

charles turned to johnny, who had remained silent and expressionless throughout charles's spiel. "and how about you, young fellow, what do you think? "

"i'm only a gambler when i need to be, myself," johnny
answered "i'm basically a religious guy."

this surprised charles a little bit but he tried not to
show it. he nodded, "i see."

"i've spent my whole life thinking about the end of the
world and the collapse of civilization," johnny
continued. "so what you say interests me. how sure
are you, of what are you telling us?"

"pretty sure," charles said, as confidently as he could.

"so why don't we go over to this place - this bank -
right now, and do it."

"it's probably closed for the night," charles answered.

"probably?" johnny raised his eyebrows. "why don't we go over and check it out. you say it's only a couple of blocks away, right?"

"he's right, boomer," magnus said. "why not check it out now? it seems a fortuitous time of night for such an undertaking. and who knows what tomorrow may bring? and if we can't get in, we can make other plans ?

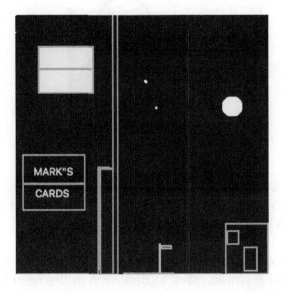

"all right," charles agreed. "in that case, there is no sense waiting around. let's get on with it."

they got up and left.

39. a sudden interruption

lord chandler suppressed a sigh. how he dreaded the next few days, with the prospect of a new war to disturb his peaceful existence.

what a damned bore mr mahmoud was! and the people he would have to deal with in the next few days as war was declared - or averted, as the case might be - would be even bigger bores, with even less polished manners.

how had he allowed himself to be ensnared in this sorry pertubation? and so close - only a few months, from his expected retirement!

how he wished he were anywhere but where he was!

how he wished he were anybody but who he was!

perhaps, lord chandler mused, some kindly souls , or desperate anarchists, will break into mrs foster's house tonight and carry me away. carry me away anywhere, so long as i do not have to deal with the likes of mr mahmoud!

he smiled inwardly at his daydreams. what was there to do but soldier on?

as lord chandler thought his thoughts, mrs foster was engaging the attention of mr mahmoud with her superlative brand of idle chatter. that, at least, was something to be grateful for.

further down the table, mary was continuing her disquisition on the early history of humankind.

"and in the empire of mu, on the other side of the earth, developments similar to those in atlantis proceeded. in atlantis the primary cause was the desire to breed strong male slaves to build a great pyramid in which to bury the great empress sophonisba, rather than to breed them to fight in the arena, but the result was the same.

in both atlantis and mu, two oppposing parties formed. in atlantis they were styled the red party and the green party, and in mu the sun party and the moon party, but the issue at debate was the same - whether the increased breeding of powerfully built male slaves rerpesented a threat to the stability of the empires.

in both ermpires, the more optimistic side pooh-poohed the idea that men, no matter how physically powerful, could ever develop the brain power, or the ability to organize themselves, to represent any threat to their female superiors.

and the other side thought it best not to tempt fate, but to be sure men remained in their inferior state, as nature intended."

mary paused, and took a sip of water.

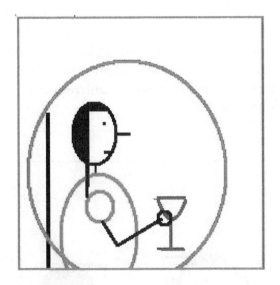

"but this is amazing!" mrs stafford exclaimed. "it explains so much!"

"it explains everything!" cried mademoiselle feval.

meanwhile, at the other end of the table, the young duke was continuing his friendly chat with joe, warning to his theme of the adventurous life..

"so," the duke was saying to joe in his most amiable manner, "just because you have never had any great adventures yet does not mean you can not have any. do you know, i think i might have just the thing for you. if you are interested, of course. what do you say?"

195

"i don't know," joe replied. "i am a little short of cash right now. i don't know if i could afford to go any adventure."

"but that is no problem!" the duke exclaimed. "just the opposite! we - uncle and i - can make it well worth your while. now - " the duke lowered his voice, although none of the other guests had been paying any attention to their conversation - "surely you have noticed the strong resemblance between us - we might as well be twins - "

but at that moment there was a loud crash from the adjoining room.

the diners all turned and beheld rogers, the under-butler, standing in the doorway with a sirrowful expression on his face.

"i am sorry to interrupt, madam, but something has come up," rogers addressed mrs foster.

behind rogers were three men in dark coats - with pistols in their hands! a large man in the center, obviously the leader, with two confederates, one of whom mrs stafford was mortified to see was mr stafford! he had a hat pulled down over his face, and she hoped that mrs foster and the other guests would not recognize him.

the big man was speaking. "i am afraid i am going to have to ask lord chandler and mr mahmoud to come with us. the rest of you just sit tight and you will be as right as raindrops. jem, check them and see if any of them are packing."

"that hardly seems likely," jeremy drawled.

"i know, but you can't be too careful."

mademoiselle feval turned to the duke, and to joe.

"can't somebody do something?" she asked.

40. one year later

it was teresa's seventeenth birthday, her day to leave mother smith's home and head out into the world, as joe had done the year before.

she had not flipped a coin, as joe had, but had decided on her own to head for the city, rather than the country.

as she walked along the highway, she wondered if she would make such a big splash in the world as poor joe had.

it did not seem likely!

the whole smith family had been astonished the year before when joe had made the lead stories in the nightly news for his heroic role in foiling the attempted kidnaping of two diplomats, lord chandler and mr mahmoud, who had been engaged in arranging the preliminaries of the newest world war.

joe had, of course, perished in his exploit, which made his story particularly interesting and sensational.

two of the persons who had, like the diplomats, survived the grisly proceedings - the young duke of dent, and a young woman named mary brown - had known enough of joe's background to give some details of it to the reporters who had flocked to the scene, and these had been picked up in the stories and headlines.

pig boy saves world!

thanks, pig boy!

yokel earns hero's laurels

some reporters found their way to mother smith's and interviewed mother and the children. one in particular, ms carlotta bligh, who had desceibed herself as "the last of the old time newshounds" had spent two whole days at the farm, interviewing everybody and promising to produce "the story of the century".

but interest in joe had quickly passed, as the new war and other events filled the news, and neither carlotta bligh's nor any of the other stories about the farm ever saw the light of day.

life at mother smith's quickly resumed its normal cycle of days and months.

now as teresa walked along, she, like joe the year before, was somewhat surprised by how few people she encountered, and how few vehicles passed by in either direction.

she saw a large woman walking about fifty yards
ahead of her.   the woman had an old-fashioned
woven basket on her left arm and teresa wondered
what was in it.

she wondered if she should try to overtake the woman
and attempt to engage her in friendly conversation.

teresa thought she felt a few raindrops.

but when she looked up there was not a cloud in the
sky.

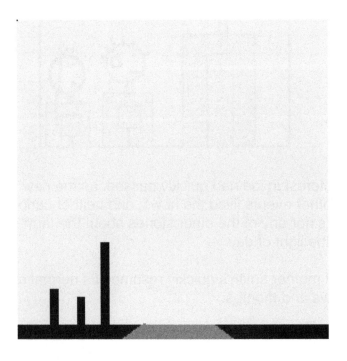

Printed in Great Britain
by Amazon

44517895R00128